D.D. Murphry, Secret Policeman

Published by Raw Dog Screaming Press
Hyattsville, MD

First Edition

A slightly different version of the chapter entitled "Change Your Mind: Case #7" originally appeared as a short story entitled "Change Your Mind" in the anthology *Portents* edited by Al Sarrantonio (Flying Fox Press)

Cover Image: Chad Savage
Book Design: Jennifer Barnes

Printed in the United States of America

ISBN: 978-1-933293-83-7

Library of Congress Control Number: 2009936200

www.RawDogScreaming.com

D.D. Murphry, Secret Policeman

by Alan M. Clark & Elizabeth Massie

Many thanks to Barbara Spilman Lawson, Jack Daves, Stephen Dale, Becky Gilberts, Elizabeth Engstrom, Cortney Skinner, Susan Stockell, Dianna Rodgers, Lorelei Shannon, Bridget McKenna, Chris McKitterick, Gene Stewart, John Helfers and Bruce Holland Rogers.

"The insane, on occasion, are not without their charms."

—Kurt Vonnegut

"People see the world not as it is, but as they are."

—Al Lee

"Reality leaves a lot to the imagination."

—John Lennon

"I believe that the moment is near when by a procedure of active paranoiac thought, it will be possible to systematize confusion and contribute to the total discrediting of the world of reality."

—Salvador Dali

"The Brain—is wider than the Sky—
For—put them side by side—
The one the other will contain
With ease—and You—beside—"

—Emily Dickinson

"The mind is its own place, and in itself, can make heaven of Hell, and a hell of Heaven."

—John Milton

His Grandmother's Eyes: Case #1

10.30 AM—Wednesday, September 13th

It was an unseasonably warm day, breezy and laced with dust and sweat. D.D. Murphry, Secret Policeman, was waiting for the bus at the corner of Seventh Avenue and Grant Street. He was on his way to the Library.

Kate, he thought. *I must see Kate. It has been almost two weeks.*

The bus arrived and Murphry climbed aboard and moved to the rear and sat where he could watch everyone. As the bus pulled into traffic, he saw a young man with a pockmarked face flash a small package of what appeared to be crack. It was obviously for the benefit of the blonde woman dressed in black leather sitting on the other side of the aisle. She sat up straight, her eyes widening as she focused on the small packet. A hungry smile brought to life the sullen features of her face.

A drug deal was about to go down, and once again D.D. Murphry, Secret Policeman, was the only witness—the only one who stood between the world of decency and those who would destroy that world with their depravity.

He checked his watch, not because he believed in the steady, inexorable flow of time—he was actually capable of stretching or compressing time for his own purposes—but because it was good procedure. 10:45 AM. He would remember that if asked for a report.

As nonchalantly as possible, he extracted from his wallet one of the many business cards he carried. Armford Brisbain, plumbing specialist. *Yes*, he thought, *I haven't used this card in a while.* He rose to his feet and proceeded up the aisle between the rows of seats, keeping his step springy, ready for anything that might happen as the bus bounded through a series of potholes on Oak Street. By the time the bumpy ride was smoothing out, he was beside the drug dealer. He leaned over, winked at the fellow and handed him the card.

"Perhaps you could use my services," he offered with a toothy smile.

The young man glared at the card and then at Murphry.

Good, Murphry thought. *Now, even if he survives, he'll never suspect I'm a Secret Policeman.*

"What's this shit?" the young man asked. "You queer or somethin'?"

But Murphry had already turned away. He made his way to the front of the bus as the vehicle picked up speed.

Fred was the driver today. Murphry knew Fred very well, having said to him "Hello," and "How are you?" and "Nice weather were having," many times, so what he was about to do would probably be pretty easy to pull off.

I just hope Fred will be able to forgive me.

At the front of the bus, he paused, and looked through the windshield. They were approaching the park. Fred always sped through the long curve beside the park, achieving speeds of up to 43 miles per hour.

Murphry was counting on it.

Just as the bus reached 42 miles per hour, Murphry leaned over and shouted in Fred's ear, "Boo!"

Fred cried out as Murphry hopped over the railing and into his lap. There was an uproar from the passengers behind him, but Murphry ignored them. He jammed his foot down onto Fred's foot over the accelerator, and the bus picked up even more speed. Murphry took control of the steering wheel, wrenching it around to the right as hard and fast as he could. The bus tumbled over onto its side and began to slide down the street. Passengers were screaming, glass shattering and metal ripping. Under it all was a powerful and satisfying grinding noise that sounded like the crime being ground off the street itself.

Murphry flew into the aisle. He closed his eyes and went limp, pretended he was drunk and oblivious to the vehicular trauma around him. After all, everyone knew that drunks survived many accidents that kill most others.

A car, its horn blaring, struck the roof and the bus came to rest.

D.D. Murphry, Secret Policeman, opened his eyes. The roof had caved in, trapping and crushing several people. Blood was everywhere. Survivors moaned, or cried out in pain. Fred, the bus driver, was still strapped into his seat, his eyes bulging and his breathing thin and labored. Looking toward the back of the bus, Murphry could see the fellow with the pockmarked face draped over one of the stainless steel supports, a large gash in his forehead. He could just make out the blonde woman tangled among a groaning pile of other passengers.

No crack for her today, he thought, with satisfaction.

"Sorry, Fred," Murphry said, but the man didn't respond. It saddened him to realize he wouldn't be seeing Fred anymore. Even if Fred survived, Murphry would not be able to ride this bus line in the future for fear of being recognized.

He looked himself over. The drunkenness technique had served him well once again. Not a scratch on him.

Sirens wailed in the distance. He knew he'd better make his escape immediately. Using his elbow, he knocked the remaining sheets of fractured windshield out of his way and stepped out of the bus.

A billboard overhead selling insurance asked him, "Are you sure you have peace of mind?"

This seemed an unusual question. *Sure I do. A few innocent people were hurt, but that's the price of freedom.*

But then, suddenly, he realized what the billboard's question was really about. He had almost forgotten his disguise.

There might be witnesses to the accident *who could describe me to the non-secret authorities! I can't risk being stopped and questioned by the cronies of the False Government. They would not find me out, (I know what I'm doing) but time would be lost. That could mean lives lost!*

Quickly, anxiously, Murphry reached into his left hip pocket, removed his comb and placed it in his shirt pocket. *It's usually the little things people noticed about you*, he thought. He knew that was true from his own observations of people.

What a way to start the week! Murphry thought. Another drug deal had been foiled, and the day was just getting started. Before beginning his career as a Secret Policeman, life had been meaningless and painful. Most of his time was spent on the street. He had been a nobody, stumbling from one inconsequential job to another.

Now life had meaning and it was all so simple. Thinking once again of the process whereby he received his missions and fulfilled his duty, pride bubbled up in Murphry's heart and gut.

"What a plan!" proclaimed a cell phone advertisement on the side of passing panel truck.

Yes, indeedy! Since no one knows I am a policeman, no one suspects I'll catch them at their dirty deeds. And since his employer, the True Government, gave him complete autonomy, he wasn't encumbered, as were the policemen in uniform, those who worked for the False Government.

Since life had not always been so good for Murphry, he was very grateful for what he had. *In fact,* he thought, *life would be just about perfect if it weren't for the False Government.* At the same time he knew that it was his battle against the evils of the False Government, that would, if he applied himself with vigor, ultimately make him lovable. Of course, his beloved Kate had a certain commitment to him, a duty and responsibility. But in order for her to truly love him, he knew he must still prove himself to her.

As the sirens became louder, Murphry made his way through the growing crowd of the curious and onto a side street. He traveled west two blocks to Lincoln and joined the small, shifting group that was waiting at the bus stop there.

As he waited, he overheard two elderly ladies talking about a young man by the name of John. "He's got his grandmothers eyes," one of the women said. "They're green with flecks of paprika." Then they smiled.

Murphry was outraged. These women looked like sweet grandmotherly types. How could they be delighted by such cruelty?

Murphry'd received information about this crime via e-mail, he realized now, but his knowledge of it was incomplete. Now, at least, he had the name *John* to associate with the crime.

His heart raced. He wanted to beat the truth out of these brutal witches. It was broad daylight, however, and there would be too many witnesses.

He reached for the stress reliever, a teaspoon, in the right pocket of his wind breaker. He'd discovered the spoon there several days ago, but didn't know how it had gotten in his pocket. He found that rubbing the ball of his thumb into the cup of the spoon lessened his tension immediately.

He scrutinized the hags, memorizing their features so he might act against them in the future.

In the meantime, he had to find this *John*. He would recover the stolen eyes and find out who John's grandmother was, just before he gave the slime ball what he liked to call justice-desserts.

He had just stored away the last details of the two witchs' features and returned to thinking about his sweet Kate at the Library when the bus arrived. He boarded and took a seat in the rear.

My superiors are doing a good job coordinating for me today.

Days like this, when everything was running like clockwork, he wished he could thank them for their efforts, but to communicate with them was to risk tipping his hand to an evildoer. No, it was best that communication with the True Government remain a one-way business. They contacted him when need be by clever, covert means. He often had to gather fragments, single words, syllables or even one letter at a time, from several text sources, to form one message. But his employer knew his mind. They used what they knew to get their ideas and information across without any misunderstanding.

He settled back in his seat and picked up a half-wrapped Twinkie from the seat beside him. It looked good, and he certainly could use the energy a little sugar would provide, but of course, it was likely left there by the False Government and therefore poisoned. He tossed it to the floor and kicked it up the aisle where it was promptly stepped on by a fat old woman who kept moving from one seat to another.

There she was again—the woman in black—in her long dark overcoat and sunglasses, standing near the entrance to the library. Although he could not see her eyes, he was sure she was watching him intently as he approached the building. Her hidden gaze sent a chill up his back and down his arms. She had been dogging him for the last few weeks. He was certain she was False Government. Who else would employ someone whose sheer existence unnerved him to the core? *She's trying to identify Secret Policemen. She will kill me if she gets the chance. Perhaps she is looking for me specifically, since I am perhaps the most important of all Secret Policemen.* He was certain she had identified him at least once, but he'd quickly altered his disguise and evaded her.

He reminded himself that his disguise was in place as he walked up the steps to the library. *She can't recognize me—she is just looking for me,* he thought, turning his face away and pretending to admire the gray stonework of the library's exterior. *I must relax so I don't raise her suspicion.* He slowed his step, popped a piece of gum in his mouth, and slowly rolled the gum wrapper into a tight little ball. He felt the woman in black's gaze upon him. She did not make any move toward him.

There. She thinks I'm just a guy enjoying his Juicy Fruit.

Even so, Murphry knew the woman in black was a problem that would not go away. He would have to find a time and place to take her out before she had the chance to make her move. *But not right now,* he told himself. *I'm in too good a mood to spoil it with violence.* To anyone listening to his thoughts this might sound like cowardice, but his mind whispered confidently, *All good crime fighters need a worthy adversary. This will be yet another chance to shine in Kate's eyes.*

Kate gave him a tired, wary look when he entered the library. She was carrying a stack of books. The muscles in her arms stood out proudly. Murphry liked what he saw.

"You again," she said, loud enough for others nearby to hear. "There are other library branches you could haunt, you know. Ones where they don't know you as well. I could show you how to get to them."

Murphry smiled and shook his head slowly as he made his way to the computers. *That's some good acting,* he thought.

Kate worked for the True Government as well. Her cover was as librarian here at the downtown branch. She and Murphry had been married in a secret, online ceremony organized by their superiors. Murphry had watched it on one of those celebrity gossip sites as a short movie clip. Of course some celebrities—movie stars, he thought, though he wasn't really up on that sort of thing—had stood in for Kate and Murphry to help keep it all a secret, but it was a lovely ceremony all the same, and Murphry cherished the memory.

It was all part of the True Government's program to encourage excellence of performance and to discourage corruption among their employees. They knew he was attracted to her. They knew that if he were paired with Kate they would be provided with invaluable leverage against any possible double dealings on Murphry's part. How could he possibly be bribed to provide aid to the False Government if he knew his employer always had the one he loved within their easy grasp? He supposed he'd resent this if he didn't trust his employer to know what was best.

Kate had to treat Murphry rudely whenever she saw him so no one would suspect they were intimate. Truth was they had yet to be truly intimate. Kate was obviously reluctant to risk breaking cover to spend time with him privately—that or she had been instructed not to. He knew she would be more willing to take that risk and incur the wrath of their employer if she truly loved him. Sure, she had respect for him as a colleague and she no doubt had profound feelings for him as well, but Murphry knew he had yet to win her deep love and the intimacy that such love implied. He was doing all he could to make that happen. Even if he did not succeed, Murphry was confident that one day his superiors would take pity on him. Perhaps they would even set up a secret conjugal visit or a romantic vacation at some exotic, hidden rendezvous.

Although she most often glowered at him and responded sarcastically when he spoke to her, Kate was capable through the amazing complexity of her voice to simultaneously provide other messages just beneath the evident disdain, a susurrus of endearments and sweet, calming language, expressions of affection, of longing and sorrow for the charade they must endure and an entreaty for him to be patient. He knew he was the only one who could hear these lovely messages.

Everyone one else probably thinks she sees me as a crazy street-person.

While Murphry waited for one of the computers to become unoccupied, he gazed at Kate as she moved around the room. She was gorgeous, with her long red hair pulled tight into a bun at the back of her head and her broad, well-padded hips and huge breasts straining at the seams of her clothing. She was what some might call frumpy from outward appearance, but Murphry knew what a delicious body she was hiding in order to maintain her cover.

She noticed him watching her. "Quit staring at me, you weirdo, or I'll have you thrown out."

And Murphry was certain that was what everyone heard, but beneath Murphry also heard, "I'm so glad to see you, my husband. Be patient with me, my dear. Like a beautiful Orchid, my love blossoms slowly. I promise that when it is in full flower, the bloom will last and last."

As she passed nearby with another stack of books, Murphry said sheepishly, "I think we could get away with meeting in the storage closet on the second floor."

"You keep it up," she said, fire in her eyes, "and I'll have you banned from this branch."

When there was no accompanying secret message, Murphry's heart took a sickening pause and he swallowed hard. She continued to glare at him for a moment, then slowly turned away. Murphry's heart was suddenly pounding in his neck.

But then he told himself, *It's okay. It's all right. She's just tired. The stress of our work and our unusual relationship has worn down her sense of humor.*

This case I'm working on, when I show her what I've done to save that poor old woman's sight, that will cheer her up. That will help prove myself to her.

Murphry's thumb had become sore. He stopped rubbing the spoon and removed his hand from his pocket. Several minutes passed before his heartbeat resumed a more normal rhythm.

Finally there was a computer free and Murphry sat to do his e-mail. He typed in his password and scanned the spam he'd received, looking for hidden meaning.

The fellow at the computer to his right was muttering under his breath. Murphry made the mistake of glancing over at him and the man turned to him.

"All this fucking junk mail!" the guy hissed. "Can't they figure out that if I don't want my penis or breasts enlarged, then I probably don't want my Peeeeeeeeeenisssssssssss and brrrrrrrreassssssssssts enlarged either? I don't want to shoot bucket-loads of cuuuuuuuuuum!"

The guy misses the point of all this, Murphry thought. That's a good thing.

"Some of their ads are filled with paragraphs of nonsense words. Its insane!"

Murphry pressed his lips together hard and nodded his head slowly to simulate sympathetic frustration, then turned back to his work.

When Murphry had first started coming to the library, before Kate had to start treating him so coldly, she had helped him set up his e-mail account. "All this spam is a nuisance," she said. "The less you give out your e-mail address the less of the stuff you'll get." But he knew what Kate was really trying to say to him: This is a way to receive covert messages from your superiors.

Murphry gave his e-mail address out freely on the web and so received a lot of junk mail filled with paragraphs of the nonsense word conglomerations. He transcribed the parts that seemed to have meaning into word processing documents in the sure and certain hope that messages from his superiors would be revealed.

Sure enough, there were always messages waiting for him. In truth they were just partial messages and it took quite a bit of work and intuition on Murphry's part to pry the relevant fragments out of the nonsense and assemble them coherently. He had to relax and work only with those words and phrases that resonated for him. Slowly but surely, each time he checked his e-mail, he would add to the assemblage until the story of a crime was revealed.

The next step was to recognize that crime in the real world. This could be difficult and frustrating, because the stories he assembled made little sense on the surface. He had to read in between the lines, think of the words as symbols, the suggestions he got from them as surreal dream stuff not to be approached with a rigid frame of mind.

If he did not recognize the events or characters in the story immediately, he had to be patient. Eventually the story would be revealed in truth in the real world. Then he could act against the perpetrator and bring succor to the victim. Thinking of this, he'd always imagined handing out suckers—lollipops—to the those who had suffered at the hands of evildoers. He was certain it would make them feel a little better.

Note to self, Murphry thought. *Buy lollipops.*

He had begun a new story this week, one that he now knew had to do with the fellow who had stolen his grandmother's eyes.

The woman at the computer to his left was wearing paisley in which Murphry read the cursive words, "They did not know to keep the truth from you."

Yes, because those dreadful harpies spoke openly about it this morning, I now have the name of the perpetrator. Perhaps I'll find another piece of the puzzle to put in place today.

Looking through his e-mails, Murphry found one strange sentence that drew his attention:

"Just because women waterproof doesn't mean swim."

He couldn't say why, but he knew this was relevant. After careful consideration, he made some important changes to the text and put it in place at the end of the story. Murphry could not explain what the message meant—not yet.

Now the crime read like this:

"The one-eyed devil only sees in one direction," his grandma would say and point out the two eggs embedded in her face. Like her words, they were round sparkling ones that bounced around in their sockets. They were god-peeping and blood-busting alive. He thought the best most people could do was paw at the dirt just inches from her face.

Along with the glossy orbs, Grandma sported six blue and purple sawmill tattoos, and her skink experiments had once saved the toenail industry. Back in the day, a mere glimpse of the bony plates of her wedding gown had caused 1920s megaphone crooners to swallow their own heads. Even when he was raised, she could still fire lap dogs from her armchair at blinding speeds. Spite for this was a waterproof woman who could not actually swim.

This was obviously the beginning of the tale of John and his grandmother's eye, a terrible crime. Murphry ached to solve it. But he saw no immediate connection between the new text he'd installed and events of which he was currently aware.

Now came his favorite part of the process of creating a coherent story. Having cut and pasted the text to form the narrative of the crime, the margin on the right of his word-processing document was ragged in appearance. He selected the text and then clicked on the command to justify the margins. In an instant all the words lined up on the right to form a straight line, like little soldiers ready for inspection. Such discipline, predictability and unquestioning simplicity.

"This should have special meaning for you," Murphry gathered from several text sources about the room.

Yes, its so much like my life, before and after, Murphry thought as he left the Library and walked the ten blocks to the Post Office. *One day I was a nothing, with little to look forward to but life on the street like some ordinary homeless guy. The next day the message that I was to become a Secret Policeman was inserted into my mind and everything became simple and clearly focused. My purpose in life defined and ensured. Justified.*

And then there was Kate.

Yes, he would eventually solve this case. It was just a matter of time. He would recover the stolen eyes and secretly send the precious orbs to Kate so that she could return them to their rightful owner. There would be no return address on the package, but she would know who they were from. Murphry kept mementos of his cases in a World-War-II ammunition box stored in a locker at the bus station, but over time he had sent Kate several of these *trophies* from the cases he solved. With such glowing evidence of his exploits to impress her, he was sure he could eventually soften her heart and win her love.

We will be happy soon. I will make sure of that.

As he entered the Post Office, he thought again of the woman in black and his swelling pride shrunk a bit. *I'll have to deal with her too,* he told himself.

Murphry got out his key and opened his P.O. box and pulled out a single envelope. It was his paycheck. How clever his employer was to make it appear to be a Social Security Disability check. It bothered him that it was always for such a small amount, but then a big Disability check might raise the suspicions of a teller at his bank.

Oh well. Pride in one's work is what's important, now isn't it?

An Arm and a Leg: Case #2

11.13 AM—Tuesday, September 25th

D.D. MURPHRY, SECRET POLICEMAN, sat on a rain-dampened bench in Roosevelt Park trying to gather his wits and organize his day, but thoughts of Kate were distracting him. He was frustrated yet again that there was no way to know exactly how Kate felt about him; no way to gauge the progress of his quest within the realm of her affections. He had always attributed her coolness to her professionalism. No other reason was tolerable to him. *More is required on my part. If I expect to be loved by her, I'd better concentrate on my work. I better find my next assignment.*

Murphry gazed sidelong at the old man on the park bench across from him. The man was wearing ordinary beige pants, tie, old man hat made of a floppy, plaid material. He had white whiskers that were trimmed unevenly, as if he did it himself and couldn't quite wrangle the clippers. His eyes were huge behind thick-lensed horn rimmed glasses. Murphry didn't know if the man was friend or foe, but at the moment that didn't matter. What mattered was the information he'd just unwittingly imparted to the secret policeman across the graveled pathway.

The old man had been talking to another old man, a bald and skinny one, a few minutes ago. They'd not come to Roosevelt Park together, but sat at opposite ends of the same park bench, at first scanning the trees and grass and then acknowledging each other with slow nods of their mottled heads. They discussed the weather, the ever-growing population of pigeons, their respective aches and pains. Then the one with the ratty whiskers pulled a newspaper from under his arm, shook it open, and proceeded to read something in the depths of the paper.

It wasn't anything the men had said about pigeons or illnesses or the dry spell the city'd been under the past week that caught Murphry's attention. It was the full-page advertisement he could see on the back page of the newspaper Ratty Whiskers was holding.

Murphry had not opened the romance novel he'd brought with him to the park. He rolled it in his hands as he read the huge block lettering of the ad.

"Furniture Shouldn't Cost You An Arm and a Leg!" declared the advertisement. "Come to Bramble Street Furniture For a Better Deal!"

Beneath the large-lettered text were scattered photos of sofas, recliners, Ottomans, and love seats. There was other text, too, giving prices and fanciful descriptions of what was just ordinary old living room furniture. Then, Ratty Whiskers shook the paper again, folded it inward, and the message was no longer visible.

But the message had been received. Obviously the store on Bramble Street was not doing so, but somewhere else in the city, another store was charging its customers arms and legs in exchange for its products.

Murphry's stomach clenched in anger. Anger at the store for taking advantage of people in such a hideous way, anger at the ignorant people who thought it was more important to have fancy furniture than one limb or another and anger at the False Government for brain-washing the populace into believing that in order to demonstrate one's worth, one needed the status symbol of brand new furniture. Was that what had happened to the men and women over at the physical rehabilitation center on the west side of town? Some of them were whole people with broken backs and broken necks, permanently attached to wheeled cots and breathing tubes. But others were missing one or more limbs. He had seen these people out on the center's grassy lawn, scooting around in fits and starts. *Darn it all!*

Murphry knew he could find the guilty furniture store. His employer wouldn't have given him such an important clue without also knowing that Murphry was the man, the Secret Policeman, to get to the bottom of it and stop the furniture store in its bloody tracks. The rage in his heart gave way to a controlled, confident energy. He stood, stuffed the paperback into the inner pocket of his jacket, rubbed his stiffened neck, and left the park.

The bus stop was just at the corner, and he knew the bus routes by heart. He'd taken them so many times he felt like he owned the vehicles and that the drivers were his personal chauffeurs. Murphry almost laughed at that thought, because in truth, they *were* his own personal chauffeurs. The buses may have belonged to a private company, but Murphry had no doubt that the drivers, as unknowing as they were to the truth of the matter, had been put into place by Murphry's employer to make sure he had a safe, reliable means of getting about town in a reasonable amount of time. Sometimes the drivers didn't turn out to be as good as they should be, and sometimes were replaced one way or other, by being fired or up and quitting. They never realized that they had been part of a bigger plan. But, their removals were part of the bigger plan, as well.

Murphry sat in the back, his hands in his pockets, counting intersections and tapping his toes, oh so quietly, inside his worn but polished shoes.

The Randolph W. Davisson Rehabilitation Center had a bright open reception lobby. Inside, a white-uniformed nurse sat at an old-fashioned oak desk, reading some sort of file. Oil portraits of stodgy old men and prudish old women of some official importance clung to the walls between polished brass sconces. If not for the brilliantly white computer on the desktop, Murphry would have thought the scene could have taken place fifteen years ago, or twenty. Stepping inside the sliding doors and stopping in the middle of the big rug with the letters RWDRC emblazoned there, Murphry felt suddenly and painfully uncomfortable. He'd never been in the center before. The smells in this place were discomforting. The sounds and the shadows made him uneasy.

The nurse put down her file, smiled an impossibly wide smile, and said, "May I help you?"

Murphry went back outside.

He stood on the sidewalk, his fingers inside his coat pocket and strumming the pages of the paperback book.

That was not good. That was stupid. I should have prepared myself before going inside.

He pulled out the book and stuck his finger between the pages randomly, knowing his employers would have a message for him about what he'd just done and how to rectify the situation. The book popped open to pages 138 and 139. His eyes scanned the print, jumping from line to line:

"Not so many women he knew drove stick shifts, but, Jake thought, this woman is a master at the throttle...."

"He tended to stay away from the tourists, but she was more beautiful than a flower in the morning sun...."

"Jake lit a cigarette and nodded. I can't imagine how much this beauty cost, he said...."

"She laughed with him, put her compact back into her purse, and said something in sweet, lilting French…."

"The truth was he'd been too busy at work to enjoy himself in the past few weeks, and the idea of spending time with her was more than pleasant."

Murphry put the book back into his pocket. The words banged against each other in his mind, until at last they settled, rearranged and trimmed, into a clear and purposeful instruction.

"The French woman with the cigarette is a master at the throttle. The truth is in her purse."

Murphry nodded slowly and intentionally, to himself and to any of the True Government who might be in various shadows across the street, peering from office building windows down the way, or watching satellite pictures captured from well above the Earth's surface. The truth was in her purse. He'd just have to find her.

He got back onto the bus and rode toward the center of town. Sitting in the back again, he stared out the window at the myriad billboards and signs and posters, all shouting to the public to buy this or that, to do this or that. "Vote for Bill Kaine!" "A Diamond is Forever!" "Burnaby's Pizza—One Taste and You'll Never Go Back!" "Winters Churn Ice Cream—As Cool and Tasty as it Gets!" The messages were for the ordinary citizen. And sometimes, they were for him. He studied each sign as the bus rambled past, but there was no new information on them concerning his current assignment.

First thing to do is find the smoking French woman at the throttle.

Throttles came with cars, Murphry was almost certain, so his first destination was the new car dealership a couple blocks from the Social Security office. It was Martins Ford, a huge, sanitary lot loaded with bright, shiny, colorful new cars, a lot that had just six months prior been a set of shabby brick apartment buildings where bums, crazies, and hookers crashed and fought and festered. Murphry knew those people well; many of them got government checks just like he did, but unlike Murphry, theirs came from the false government for doing absolutely nothing—that, or they were being paid to be a nuisance. Most of the bums, crazies, and hookers had moved on down the street a bit to take up in an abandoned warehouse by the river. Murphry didn't hate them, he just didn't think too much of them. They were clueless. He was clued. He had a purpose. They did not. That was the way of the world.

One of the salesmen saw Murphry at the edge of the lot, and strode forward with one hand out and a lock-jawed grin slashing the lower portion of his face. As he got closer to Murphry, however, the hand drew back slightly and the grin faltered and folded. Murphry knew he looked normal in his powder blue leisure suit, his newly buffed loafers, and his freshly combed hair, but maybe he looked a bit angry. As a Secret Policeman, he knew he felt and sometimes even looked intimidating. Murphry puffed his cheeks slightly in an attempt to look demure.

"Ah, can I help you, sir?" said the salesman. He squinted as though the sun was in his eyes, though it wasn't. It was a very cloudy day. Murphry only said, "Id like to talk to your smoking French saleswoman."

The man's brows went up, and his face went lopsided for a minute. Then he said, "What? Oh, we don't have one of those, but we have some hot cars, fresh off the line…."

"No, thank you," Murphry said. He left Martins Ford and spent the rest of the day exploring the other dealerships in the city. By 9 PM, he'd visited all of them, and none had a female French employee, though they did have a lot who smoked.

It had been a long day. Murphry walked down to one of the better shelters, frustrated that he'd gotten nowhere on his assignment. He had to find the truth so he could stop that cruel furniture store from its ghastly trade of leather and cloth for flesh and bone. At the reception desk he signed in, found an empty cot near the back of the large room, and curled up holding his shoes. He stared at the ceiling, watching the patterns made by the shadows of smelly men getting up and down out of their cots, to vomit, piss, or take a dump in the bathroom down the hall. Life as a Secret Policeman was difficult, but Murphry never doubted the magnitude of his calling. He never buckled under the weight of the responsibility on his shoulders.

In the morning, he joined the other men at the large folding tables for a breakfast of oatmeal, coffee, and cantaloupe slices. He bowed his head as the preacher—it was a religious shelter, with the dining hall walls all painted up with bruised Jesuses, fluffy sheep, blood-drenched crosses, and wall-eyed angels—said the blessing, and then he quickly downed the food.

Back on the street, he felt ready to face the brisk autumn day. He had bathed at the shelter, had brushed his teeth with a toothbrush the church members had given him, and combed his hair with his favorite comb. The toothbrush was discarded in a roadside trash bin beneath some worm-laced Chinese carry-out. It wouldn't do to have too much DNA lying around for whoever might think it useful. The comb went into the hip pocket of his trousers.

Taking a deep breath of cold, exhaust-filled air, Murphry turned north and walked to the library. It was time to trade the romance paperback for another at the library's paperback trading bin. He hoped he would see his wife, Kate, even though he would not be able to stay long enough to sit and watch her stack books and chase loud teenagers outside. He felt a movement in his groin as he imagined her long red hair shaken free of its bun, her large breasts popping free of the cotton fabric of their restraints.

No, stop it, he chastised himself as he shouldered his way through the sliding front doors and slipped left to the paperback bin near the copy machines. *I know she's enjoyed the few treasures, the few spoils, that I've sent to her. She cannot speak of them to me, but I know she is as secretly pleased with the gifts as I am to offer them. And soon, with all I've done, she will fall deeply in love with me.*

But for now, he would have to be content to scan the faces in the library until he spotted her lovely countenance, and watch with deep love as she bared her teeth in his direction.

Murphry moved his hand over the jumbled pile of paperbacks—clearly his dear Kate had not had time to straighten them up yet—until his fingertips brushed the top of a thin, creased volume. He picked it up and put the romance in its place. He did not need to look at the title; it was what was inside that mattered. He pocketed the book, glanced back to see the beautiful Kate directing an elderly lady toward the reference area, and went out to the street.

There was a hissing sound outside, and Murphry couldn't pin down where it was coming from. *Hsssssssss........*

Hssssssss........

Like someone passing air through his teeth, like static on a television set, like wind through trees. *Hsssssss.*

What does it mean?

Murphry looked at the other side of the street, which was lined with a shoe shop, clothing store, and bookstore. Two young ladies stood on the sidewalk in front of the clothing store, shopping bags and purses smashed beneath their arms. A disgruntled toddler pulled on one of the women's legs. A teenaged boy elbowed past them, deep in a tune on his headphones. The young ladies shifted away, revealing the whole of the clothing store's plate glass window. Murprhy's gut clenched. The woman was there, behind the glass. The tall woman in black. Sunlight and swirling exterior reflections shrouded her face, but her fingers seemed to strum the air as if reaching for him. She'd identified him again. He had not evaded her as he'd thought he had. The skin of Murphry's arms prickled beneath his shirtsleeves. The darkness of her clothing might not arouse suspicion in the ordinary populace, but Murphry saw the meaning there. She wore her dark purpose proudly, arrogantly. She was the False Government's latest tool for rooting out Secret Policemen.

Since many of the crimes Murphry and his colleagues fought against were a result of activities and goals of the False Government—drug trafficking, nourishment fraud, medical extortion and malice, brainwashing through language manipulation and peer comparison escalation—they were always trying to identify the Secret Policemen. He used to believe they did this with simple assassination in mind, but with the advent of the woman in black he suspected their purpose was much darker.

Turning his head, he looked for a lamppost or signpost to slip behind in order to disguise himself. There was nothing within easy reach. His teeth bore down together, making a little crunching sound. He looked back at the plate glass window. The woman was no longer there.

Good. That's good. Maybe turning at a certain angle made her think I'm not who I am. Maybe position can be a disguise sometimes.

A jogger raced along the curb in front of Murphry, his arms and bony knees pumping. Cars slowed down and stopped, waiting for their green light.

Hssssss.

What was that sound? Was it from the street, or was it sent into his mind from his employer? Murphry walked half a block north and glanced into the narrow alleyway there. He spied a police clean up crew hosing down a bloody spot back near a pile of dented cardboard boxes. The water hissed from the hose. Murphry rubbed away the line of snot that had formed beneath his nose in the cold.

What does the hiss mean?

Murphry slipped away from the alley, leaned against the brick wall of a stationery store, and opened the paperback. The contents dealt with raising small livestock. Didn't matter. There was more for him here than stock trailers, grain bins, and hog wallows. Murphry let his eyes skim the pages that had fallen open. The important words leapt out at him, words separated by other words and punctuation. Yet in his mind they came together as a whole. An entire message. A priceless clue.

"Only…the machine that runs…without gasoline…will hold…information…for those who…seek…the female pig…when the time has come…around to…open the barn door…that is…latched. A sow will utter a prolonged "wee"… in the late night…after new bedding is laid…but rust will flake…and…rain can destroy…all previous efforts."

Murphry let out the breath he'd been holding. He patted his pocket for his spoon, dipped his hand inside, and began to stroke the slick metal. Somehow he'd gotten blood on it, his or someone else's he couldn't tell. He could feel the blood on it and that was troubling, but as he rubbed it, his heart, which had picked up a quick and uncomfortable rhythm, was calmed.

The machine that runs without gasoline? What could that be? Something that ran by battery? Lots of things ran by batteries. Clocks, flashlights, remote controls.

But it had to have some sort of throttle. And it had to hiss.

Murphry walked toward Roosevelt park as he let the words roll back and forth in his mind. He had his assignment, and had to act quickly so no more witless people would be mutilated. Yes, even the stupid deserved his protection. In the park, he paced back and forth, back and forth. Throttle. Female pig. "Wee." Rust. *Hssssss.*

Rust. Rusting. Rustle. Rustburg. Rustburg. Where had he seen that name before? Yes, he remembered. There was a Rustburg Road.

Murphry hopped onto a bus at the park and stared at the map near the ceiling. There it was, Rustburg Road. A street on the northern outskirts of town, near the city dump. This bus wouldn't take him there, but there might be a connection, the way it looked on the map. Murphry almost asked the bus driver but then bit his lip and remained silent. No good to let the driver, as unknowing as the man might be, have an inkling as to what Murphry was up to.

Two buses and a half-mile walk later, Murphry stood in a shabby, 1950s-era suburb at the corner of Rustburg Road and September Drive. The road was a short one, ending in a cul-de-sac. Who was he looking for on Rustburg Road? A pig? No. A barn?

Maybe. Some of the houses had aluminum sheds out back, and a few had weather-worn wooden structures. Murphry felt for the paperback book in his jacket pocket and to his horror, discovered it had fallen out somewhere back in the bus. He grabbed the spoon instead, and began thumbing it rapidly. Then he walked up the street, looking to both sides, on the look-out for his new clue. It had to be here.

In one yard, a young woman stood with her shovel, chopping a cluster of dead black-eyed Susans from a garden patch. A toddler sat in the grass beside her, picking withering dandelions and sticking them into her mouth. In a second yard, two dogs attached to chains lunged and snapped. A third and fourth were empty, and in a fifth, a rusty car sat on a grass-punctured concrete driveway in front of a portable carport.

Rust.

Murphry stopped and stared. Another rust. This had to be the place.

There was a ramp to the front door stoop and another to the door beneath the carport, and Murphry knew what ramps meant. They meant wheelchairs. Wheelchairs probably had throttles, the electric ones, anyway. *Yes, yes!*

Murphry scanned the street to make sure no one was watching, and he sneaked into the yard and across the carport to squat between a tall plastic trash bin and a stack of old wooden pallets. He gave his spoon one more rub and then put on the wool gloves he kept in his pants pocket.

She didn't come outside until it was late in the afternoon and Murphry felt he was developing frost on his chin. She was middle-aged and chubby, with a heavy fall jacket and a black purse clutched to her breasts. She maneuvered the electric wheelchair down the short ramp, muttering to herself as she went. "Damn Brenda, callin' me so late in the day, sayin' oh, oh, come over Mama, the baby's done gone and got herself a earache and I gotta get her some medcine. She keep a hat on that baby, she wouln' get no earache!"

Murphry watched the woman as she steered her hissing vehicle around the car to the driver's side and grappled with the latch, popping open the door. Then he sneaked up on her from behind as she was preparing to hoist herself from the chair into the car seat. He saw that her right foot was in a cast.

I'll bet she is missing part of her foot! She's maimed!

Murphry spun the wheelchair around so the woman was facing him. He expected her to complain initially, but not really scream, as he knew his appearance was not threatening. He only wanted to talk to her, after all. But she did neither complain nor scream. She merely hitched her lip and said, "You that man Brenda sent over to do my mulchin'? Well, you sure are late for yard work, ain't ya? The 'quipments in the tool shed back of the house. Ain't got no lock on it, so you can just get it out and get started. I want a nice, thick pile of mulch around my bushes, not like last year when there wasn't more than an inch or two put down an a couple of em died of the cold."

Murphry said, "Are you French?"

The woman blinked, drew back slightly, and said, "Why, you don't talk English?"

"What's your name?"

The woman scowled, scratched her chin, and said, "I'm Marie Garringer. You know that. Brenda told you where I live and you found me."

"Marie's a French name, isn't it?" asked Murphry. "And French people say, wee."

"Wee? What?"

"It means yes. Wee. Do you smoke?"

"Now, that ain't none of your business," said Marie. She reached for her toggle switch to turn her chair around but Murphry held it tightly. "Let me loose, boy."

"I need to know if you smoke." Murphry tried to be polite but the woman was standing, or sitting, in the path of justice. That wouldn't do. "Tell me."

The woman slapped at Murphry's hands but he didn't let go of the chair. "What is wrong with you? Brenda said you did good work, but it looks like she sent me a damned idiot!"

"Please show me what's in your purse, Ma'am." Maybe calling her ma'am would help ease her worries.

But it didn't, and she struggled, and Murphry struggled harder. The chair whipped back and forth and around, Murphry grabbing for the purse with one hand and clutching the arm of the chair with the other; the woman clawing at Murphry with both hands and chopping the air with her teeth.

And then somehow, Murphry snatched the seat of the chair and it flipped over backward and the woman's head hit the concrete driveway with a decided "smack." Her eyes rolled up and she didn't move any more or say anything else. One of the small front wheels on the chair spun three times and then stopped.

Murphry sighed, shook his head, and moved the plastic trash barrel in front of the woman to help conceal her. Then he took the purse from her loosened fingers. Inside, he found a pack of gum, a pack of cough drops, and a pack of matches.

Matches, Murphry thought. *She smokes!*

He dug deeper. The truth is in her purse. So were her house keys. He unlocked the door and slipped inside. Where had she traded her foot for her furniture?

There was a shabby set in the living room. She could have had it ten years or more, so that wouldn't tell him what he needed to know. But then in her bedroom he spied a lovely new cedar chest beneath the window. He clawed open the lid. The scent of an evergreen forest rose to his nostrils along with the smells of old postcards and photographs. The somewhat blurry photograph on top was of a woman dressed in black, wearing sunglasses and a dark hat, standing beside a sleek new sports car. She looked younger here, but then people often changed to a more flattering look when being photographed.

So, the woman in black was mixed up in this all along. And, fearing no retribution, she shamelessly left her calling card in the trunk she traded for the poor woman's foot! Just what power does she hold in the False Government? What exactly is her role?

The only thing written on the back of the photo was the words *My Jaguar*. Murphry looked around the interior surface of the chest. On the inside of the lid was a paper label. "Newton's Home Furnishings."

That was it. The place. The clues all came together. Murphry knew where he was to go now, and what he was to do next. First, though, a trophy from this case to send to Kate. Murphry peeled the Newton's Home Furnishings label off and put it in his pocket. Then he went back outside, fished the matches from the Frenchwoman's purse, a small can of charcoal lighter fluid from her unlocked tool shed, and headed back into the city.

Fragment: Eat My Words

1:22 PM—Thursday, October 15th

D.D. MURPHRY, SECRET POLICEMAN, sat under a tree in Roosevelt Park, trying to relax and take a little time off from his work.

There was a group throwing a baseball to his left, a disheveled elderly fellow, standing on a park bench, preaching the gospel to no one in particular, to his right. The subject of his sermon was the Devil's insidious plot involving the theory of evolution. "God and the Devil are even now doing battle in our courts over this issue," the preacher said.

The truth was that Murphry could not relax. Having not received any messages from his employer in over a week, he was between assignments and had little to do but worry. He feared that since he had not heard from his employer for so long, he had been secretly fired or that words had abandoned him and would no longer facilitate his communication with the True Government. If this were true, it would mean that he had lost Kate as well.

These were not new fears, but he had never felt them this intensely. He had experienced lapses in communication before, times when text meant little more than what one could read on the surface, but never for so prolonged a period. This after nearly three weeks in September when absolutely everything seemed to make sense and everything went his way. Such heady times never lasted, however. Murphry reminded himself that the lapses in communication came and went the same way and never lasted for long, but those times were quite sobering and depressing. Little seemed to make sense. If he searched for hidden meaning, his imagination got the better of him and the messages he found were ominous warnings without context.

There was no way of knowing for sure, but Murphry suspected that the woman in black might be the cause of the current loss of communication. Whenever he saw her and she seemed to be looking at him (he was never certain she was looking directly at him because of her dark glasses) he felt as if a vacuum had been turned on, one that sucked up not only his image, his movements and activities, but something of his personality as well. Perhaps even her dark clothes were designed to soak-up energy *and* information. And what was she doing with all that information if not analyzing it to determine what his role was within the True Government and what he was up to? He was fairly certain that she was not sucking in his thoughts, or she'd have found him out long ago. But perhaps the messages the True Government meant for him were being stolen by the woman in black before they could reach Murphry. Perhaps she needed only to be within a certain proximity to him to disturb communications. She was probably getting nothing from the messages as they were coded and tailored for his mind, but the thought of it was unnerving to him nevertheless.

To alleviate his anxiety and depression, Murphry needed to get his mind off these thoughts. He needed distraction. He dug a biology magazine, taken from a recycling bin on the street, out of his backpack, opened it and began doing the crossword puzzle.

1-Across—Mutually beneficial relationship between two different species—nine letters.

He filled in the nine squares with the word, "mutualism."

Murphry knew something special about words. Words were alive and, he hoped, they were his friends. At least they had been up until a week ago. This was because he had always maintained a good relationship with them, spending most of his evenings in the cold winter months reading in the library. He knew that if words were kindly disposed to you, they were willing on occasion to become subordinate to your will. If not, they revealed your true intentions to others without you knowing about it. While talking about one thing, your words might express something else. While the expression has it that "actions speak louder than words," Murphry knew that was only true of people who didn't maintain a good relationship with words.

Obviously, the True Government maintained a good relationship with words as well. If that weren't so, communication between Murphry and his employer would not be nearly so effective. Perhaps, Murphry thought, the relationship between words and the True Government might be strained at times. That might account for the periods of poor communication.

All the more reason to relax, Murphy counseled himself. *If the lapse is caused by the woman in black or hard feelings between the True Government and words, then it has nothing to do with me.* Although none of these eventualities was a good thing, Murphry was somewhat comforted by the thought.

"If you have been tempted to follow the ways of science and have strayed from your faith," shouted the preacher, "know that faith is the condition of unquestioning belief. You have but to believe that Jesus died for your sins and you shall not perish. Read the word of God, then look into your hearts and you will know the truth."

Yes, Murphry thought, *there is truth in words, but you have to respect words and allow them to do their work.* In addition to receiving messages from his superiors through available text sources, Murphry allowed language to inform his thought processes both intellectually and emotionally. He did this by maintaining a sort of free association, moment to moment, with whatever text was available, the book he carried or any text that might appear within his environment, thereby occasionally receiving messages even when no one was sending them.

He had taken up this practice after witnessing those who preached the Bible. If ever a preacher needed something to say, whatever his or her agenda, inspiration for it could be found in the Bible. Therefore, the words themselves must be saying something to the preachers, something personal and tailored just for them.

Since there was so much poetry to the text of the Bible, Murphry discovered that he, too, could find whatever meaning he wanted within it. It was like finding animals in the amorphous shapes of clouds. No wonder there were so many different Christian religions, and no wonder Christians thought they needed the preachers to tell them how to believe.

Murphry had carried a Bible with him for over a year until it was stolen, but paperback novels and instruction manuals seemed to do the trick just as well.

1-Down—Community of decentralized leadership—four letters.

The four-letter boxes crossed the word, mutualism, offering "i" as the second letter.

Murphry completed the word *hive.*

Perhaps words are a sort of hive intelligence. Even though each word performs a different function, they don't thrive and operate independently, but are reliant upon the entire community for support in order to survive, something like the Portuguese man-of-war.

Most people consider the Portuguese man-of-war a jellyfish, but Murphry had learned that each was a community made of single-cell organisms. Some of the organisms provided structure, some aided in locomotion, some digestion, some reproduction, but they functioned as one. Sort of like nouns, adjectives, adverbs, prepositions and so forth.

Yes, it is the community of... language.

"Science is the root of all of society's ills. The Devil continues to tempt us with the fruit of knowledge."

He refers to the fruit of the tree of knowledge of good and evil, Murphry thought. He wanted to correct the preacher, but didn't want to speak. Religion wasn't important to him. He went back to his crossword puzzle.

2-Across—Species of polyps living in "hard-rayed" calcium carbonate structures—twelve letters.

The twelve boxes crossed the word, hive, at the letter "e." Murphy knew the crossword puzzle was referring to coral, but had no idea what the answer was to this question because he didn't know the species name.

Perhaps language was more like a community of coral polyps in that it needed a boney house in which to live. Could be language's boney home was Mankind. Just as coral polyps created the hard structures in which they lived, had language created mankind?

This was a frightening thought. Was language just using him? What would happen once it didn't need him any more? Was the silence he had been experiencing an indication that that time had come?

No, that is your imagination speaking. Relax.

Murphry took several deep breaths and tried to concentrate on the crossword puzzle. He rubbed the spoon in his pocket. He skipped 2-Down and 3-Across because he didn't understand the questions.

"Of course it is all a part of God's plan," the preacher said. "Yes even the evil one is a part of His plan. You cannot enter the Kingdom of Heaven without first having survived the trials of the Devil."

4-Across—Mutualism between algae and fungus—six letters.

Wait a minute—there's a message here in the words of this puzzle. Murphry felt a thrill at the possibility there was a message being conveyed. Perhaps his fears of abandonment had been for no reason once again.

Murphry wrote the word, "lichen," in the squares.

A mutually beneficial symbiosis, Murphry thought. *The fungus part of the lichen gives it structure while the algae part allows it to process energy through photosynthesis.*

The True Government was indeed trying to communicate with him. He could feel the smile growing on his face.

Civilization wouldn't exist without language, so human beings are benefiting immensely. And what does language get out of it? Perhaps we provide mobility.

There was definitely a message here, but it was vague—probably just something his employer wanted him to think about. He imagined himself shouting for joy, but knew he could never do that.

Is language an alien life form? Perhaps language became stranded on Earth at some point in the distant past. They chose a life form—Man—as a vehicle in which to return to the stars. Language is changing us and directing our efforts, slowly, subtly, influencing our thoughts and desires toward this goal. It is nothing to be afraid of. To the contrary, it is perhaps how we have arrived at civilization.

That is why language has been my ally. Language supports the rule of law, the basic underpinning of our society. Since I represent law and order, I have had the support of all words.

"The Bible is the Word of God," the preacher shouted. The strain of his shouting was beginning to tell on him and lent a desperate tone to his voice. "You may not believe now, but one day you shall. Do not wait until it is too late!"

Perhaps language is after all one entity with many specialized limbs. Could it be that language is God, and that is why people respond so strongly to religious texts of all sorts. Or is it just that people respond so strongly, so emotionally to the ideas and concepts expressed by language that they are easy to convince of almost anything, including the existence of a god. Everyone wants to make sense of things, but that doesn't mean they are any good at it.

Murphry tried to keep an open mind. There were plenty of concepts, such as telekinesis, God, ESP, witchcraft and UFOs, for which he held no belief or disbelief. They occupied a shelf in his mind—one in clear view—that he added to from time to time. He imagined a label hanging from the shelf that read, "Not enough evidence." Today he placed on the shelf the information he'd received via the crossword puzzle and his resultant speculations about language. He was comfortable not deciding just yet if there was any truth there, but he felt confident that eventually evidence would surface to support one or more of the ideas.

Time will tell.

The sermon broke up as the preacher began to cough. After a rather painful sounding coughing fit, he gave up on it. He mumbled, "Please forgive me, Father," stepped down from his bench, lit a half burnt cigarette and walked away.

The rest of the crossword puzzle had nothing to offer Murphry—either he couldn't understand the questions or he didn't know the answers.

Murphry looked around to see if he could spot the woman in black. If she were watching him, she might have realized from the expressions on his face that he'd received a message from his superiors. *That's all she'll get out of me*, he thought defiantly as he tore the puzzle out of the magazine and ate it.

With a spring in his step, he headed out of the Park, confident that he'd be receiving a new assignment from the True Government any moment.

Head on a Platter: Case #3

11:25 PM—Saturday, November 2nd

D.D. MURPHRY, SECRET POLICEMAN, was hiding. He didn't often hide; there was no need. As a Secret Policeman he had his manner, his words, his actions and his disguises down pat. Who would ever suspect him? But on the street corner, the woman in black had spoken to him.

He had not seen her coming until it was too late. He'd been picking a particularly itchy rash of scabs from off his knuckles. At first he'd wondered, as the dried brown blood flaked away, if there was a message in the jagged shape of the finger wounds, gained when he'd tripped on a rough patch down by the river, but there wasn't, unless it was Chinese or Sanskrit and he didn't know Chinese or Sanskrit and he knew his employer knew he didn't know Chinese or Sanskrit.

She'd come up from his left side and it wasn't until he heard her hiss that he snapped to attention and spun about. He could see himself reflected in her giant black glasses.

"I think you know what I want," she said in a dark and hideous voice.

And he did. And he ran. He made it around an alley corner, just in time to throw on a disguise by flipping up his collar and untying his shoes. Then he took a breath and strolled out the other side of the alley. A block later, he stopped and looked back and she was not there. He raced ahead to the Henley Street Laundromat to hide from the woman in black. He hoped she could not smell his trail.

It had been more than two hours now and she had not shown up. He had sat there with his flipped up collar and untied shoes, hands gripping his knees, holding still, waiting, as customers chatted and argued and crammed clothes into washers and dragged balls of clothes out of dryers. The woman in black's attempt on his life, or worse, had been thwarted.

It was late. The Laundromat would close in thirty-five minutes. He liked the place and had been there many times. Not doing clothes, of course, because he washed his clothes every few weeks at the shelter. No, he liked to sit in the laundromat on occasion because it was a place where his mind, for a brief time, could take a short break from the constant input of the True Government and the noisy assault of the world at large. He could sit on a scratched plastic chair, listen to the *thwump-thwump* of the dryers, the fussing of the babies, the arguing of the children, and the chatter of the men and women who got together over baskets, detergents, and quarters.

Thinking of that reminded him to get up and look around. Murphry frequently found stray quarters under the chairs and machines. One time he found a five-dollar bill, soaked and plastered on the inside of a washing machine lid. Tonight he found thirty-seven cents. It was a sign from the True Government that he had a right to be there, to rest a little, as unnoticed as a matchless sock or tattered towel. He took his seat again.

The customers drifted away, out the doors, into the heavy, sleet-threatening night.

Murphry looked at his reflection in the greasy glass of the huge windows. Past his distorted face, headlights swirled and streetlights pulsed, making a peaceful, silent dance in the dark. He watched himself take his spoon from his pocket and rub it—he still couldn't figure out how he'd gotten blood on it—then put it back. He tried a smile, but in the warped glass it was more of a sneer, so he closed his lips. Then, from the depths of the same pocket, he retrieved a handful of linty peanuts he'd been saving since lunch, and put them in his mouth one at a time. He tapped his incisors on each in turn, as if warning the nut it was time to die, and then flicking it back to his molars for the crushing blow. Peanuts were like citizens in the jaws of a False Government. A nice, warm, comfortable place to float along without a care, until *snap*. They never knew what hit them.

The Laundromat door blew open, letting in an angry young woman in a royal blue suit and beige overcoat. She was followed by a companion, a middle-aged man in pinstripe, who carried a pillowcase as if it were a soiled diaper. Both glanced at Murphry on his plastic chair near the window, rolled their eyes, and returned their attention to each other.

"That asshole idiot," seethed the woman.

That voice! The anger! Just to see her, hear her made Murphry want to curl into a ball and die. *Could this be the woman in black in disguise?* To get up and leave, Murphry would have to walk by her and that would only draw attention to himself.

He hunkered down in his seat. If she were the woman in black, she didn't seem to recognize him, so his own disguise was holding. Perhaps without her black clothing to aid her surveillance, her ability to spot him was diminished.

Her jaw was set and her eyes were narrowed. "We don't get paid enough to wash his fucking, puked-on shirt. What the hell was he thinking, getting into a drinking contest the night before our big presentation? Here we are, in some BFE city for a sales conference neither you nor I wanted to go to with asshole Clark at the helm, and he decides he can out-drink a bunch of locals who looked like they lived at that damned pub! God, Paul, we should just take it back and tell him we couldn't find anywhere to wash his shirt. Let him smell like vomit tomorrow morning and let the mountain crash down right on his big, fat ass!"

I cannot know for certain if she is the woman in black. However, this angry woman is obviously on an evil mission of her own. I will observe her for a while to see what she's up to.

Paul tossed the pillowcase on top of a washer. He sniffed, then dug in his pants pocket and retrieved several coins. Murphry watched out of the corner of his eye while pretending to read a "Safe Clothes Washing and You" poster on the wall.

"Got quarters," the man said simply.

The woman put her hands on her hips and shook her head. "It's freaking cold outside! And yet, here we are, like two stupid, trained walruses…"

Don't you mean trained seals? Murphry thought.

"I think you mean trained seals," said Paul.

Murphry clamped his mind shut before Paul read anymore from his thoughts.

"You don't train walruses," the man went on. "They'd kill you as sure as look at you."

"Whatever," said the woman. "We aren't his trained seals or his trained walruses! But we're acting like it. Clark pukes, goes to his room, gives you his shirt, and demands that you get it clean and dry by morning. And there you are, not knowing a washing machine from an espresso machine…"

"I do know a walrus from a seal."

"Yes, okay, but you bang on my door when I'm getting ready to go to bed and insist I help you wash the man's shirt! Why the hotel can't get one vomit-shirt cleaned by 9 AM is beyond me. Why Clark only brought one dress shirt on this trip is beyond me. Why Clark can't get his drunken ass down the street to find a coin laundry is also beyond me. And why you and I both agreed to do it for him is way beyond me!"

Paul shrugged. "He's the son of the company's owner."

"Yeah, well, he's more like an asshole. A major shit-lazy *creephole*! Makes me work overtime when he knows my girl Hannah's home, hoping to see her mother at least once a week in the freaking daylight hours. I may look like a high-powered corporate bitch-in-the-making and maybe I am, but when it comes to my kid, I'd rather be having a tea party with plastic cups than sipping office coffee in Styrofoam once six PM has come and gone." The woman then looked at Murphry as if she thought he, himself, were vomit on a plastic chair. "Take a picture," she said with a scowl. "It'll last longer."

Murphry looked away, said, "I don't have a camera."

"Incredible!" The woman spun back to Paul.

"Okay, listen," she said. "It'll take for fucking ever to run that thing through the machine. You hand-wash it and we'll toss it in the dryer for twenty minutes. Take it out quickly and it shouldn't have too many wrinkles. Look, there's a machine where you can get a little box of detergent for a dollar and a half." She crammed a dollar bill and two quarters into the slot, banged the tab, and a little box dropped into the receptacle. She snatched it out, strode to men's bathroom, and gestured impatiently for Paul to join her. "Go in there and put this thing in the sink. Hot water, are you listening?"

"Yeah." Paul put his hands into his pocket.

"Hot water. Use all this detergent. Scrub the thing, get out all those…chunks. Don't take too long, though, this dump closes at midnight."

"Why don't you scrub it in the women's room?"

"Because Clark told you to do it! You're lucky I got dressed to come out here in the first place. I tell you, tomorrow morning when the board members are on hand to hear our reports, I'm going to give them a private earful about Clark's incompetence and arrogance. I'm going to have Clark's head on a platter, as sure as you please."

Murphry almost choked on an un-chewed peanut. He put one hand in the pocket with the spoon and nuts, the other in the pocket where he carried his curly-paged paperback western novel. Beneath his fingers, he could feel the words on the pages, pulsing, breathing, demanding him to take it out and find instruction.

Paul grabbed the restroom door handle and yanked it open. Murphry darted for the Laundromat door and pushed outside into the cold. A brisk wind caught the back of his neck and crawled up into his hair. He watched through the glass, watched the woman kick at a dust ball on the floor and shake her head. Then he ran around to the back of the building.

He knew the Laundromat. He'd come here for a long time, and was aware that one of the windows to the back storeroom would come up with the right jiggling of the frame. It could have something to do with the fact that the building was old, a brick 1940's era flat-top, but also the fact that Murphry had tampered with the window several weeks ago when the science fiction novel he'd selected to carry with him had fallen through a huge hole in his pocket and had been left behind. The building didn't have a security alarm…it was just a coin op laundry, for heaven's sake, and it didn't take much to break the latch, shove open the window, and crawl in to get the book. Thank the True Government the book was still there. He'd then gone to the library and left his holey pocket jacket on a chair near the front desk, hoping Kate would see it, see the need, and take it into her little librarian's office behind the front desk and secretly sew it up. It would have been so nice, being able to reach into his pocket to feel not only the book but the threads she had so lovingly put into place. Of course she didn't do that—not because she didn't love him (he was sure that her affection for him was growing), but because she could not take that chance. All she did was stuff the jacket into the trash bin beside the copy machine. Murphry got it back out again before the janitor made his rounds. He then stitched up the hole himself back at the shelter. But Kate had touched the jacket in the only way she really could without revealing anything to the library patrons and staff. He'd slept with it under his head that night.

The back window of the Laundromat slid open with a few grunts and thwacks from the heel of Murphry's hand. As he hoisted himself up, he noticed what looked like gang graffiti spray painted on the brickwork next to the window. "BR's Live! GTS's DIE!" He hesitated, his feet dangling, his hands on the scabby windowsill paint and his arms locked, and thought, "die." *Yes, die!* The paint wasn't really a gang marking. The True Government had put that there to let him know that if he didn't act quickly in regards to the woman in the Laundromat, someone would DIE. And that would be die with all caps. No simple death, but something hideous and bloody. Murphry's stomach clenched. He crawled inside, pulled the window down, and moved to the door, keeping quiet, hiding. A slice of light pooled from beneath, and he could hear Paul and the woman talk.

"Aren't you done in there?"

"Almost."

"We're going to get locked in here, you don't move your ass."

A door opened and slammed shut. There were footsteps out in the washer room. "Here. Throw it in the dryer. Haven't you ever been to a coin laundry before?"

A dryer door opened, closed. Coins clicked and rattled. Then the machine started up. *Thwump-thwump-thwump-thwump.* Not so loud with only one shirt. A plastic chair scraped the floor. The woman said, "You're going to sit on that thing? Do you know how many diseased asses have sat on that thing?"

"Enough, Robin."

Robin. So that was her name. The woman who would have a man's head on a platter for only wanting a clean shirt. Sons whose fathers owned companies should have clean shirts. Murphry pressed his forehead against the door and squeezed his ears to hear more clearly.

"Tomorrow, Paul, and you back me up, you come with me when we have a little private chat with Anderson. We're going to spill all the beans. Sexual harassment, favoritism, doctoring of the books."

"I'm not so sure he's ever doctored the books."

"He probably has! Revenge is going to be sweet."

Paul grunted something Murphry couldn't hear. There was a long period where neither talked, but shadows moved back and forth beneath the door, strobing the light.

Head on a platter.

Die.

Clark, son of the company's owner, was going to be decapitated.

But not if D.D. Murphry did his job.

Squatting down for as much illumination as possible, Murphry pulled out the western novel. The pages were shadowed in gray and the words hard to decipher, but he pressed his face close. Poor lighting couldn't stop him from his duty, though complete sentences wobbled and floated on the page and it was impossible to read one whole. His eyes slid around the jimble-jumble, picking up "fevered passion," "filth," "baby carriage," "sweat-slicked bicep," "silvery ocean." With a topless ballpoint pen from his shirt pocket he noted the words in order on the inside cover of the book. *Fevered passion. Filth. Baby carriage. Sweat-slicked bicep. Silvery ocean.*

What was he to do with this? There was not enough information here! His mind raced, then he shook his head. He was afraid…afraid this assignment would slip through his fingers for lack of enough clues. If that occurred, what would happen to him? Would his own boss have his head on a platter? What would Kate think?

Stop it. You'll find the answers. You always do. You know how this works.

He put the pen and book back into his pocket and listened at the door, tuning his ear to register soft sounds above the thunder-heavy pounding of his heart.

After a silent ten minutes or so, the dryer door opened with a soft metallic clunk. The thwumping stopped. Robin said, "All right, it's dry." Silence. Then, "I've folded it as good as a little ole maid would have done. Now let's get back to the fucking hotel and present the bosshole with his shirt. Tomorrow, we'll present him with a hell of a lot more."

Footsteps retreated. A soft whoosh indicated they'd pushed through the door. Murphry scrambled out the back window, cutting his shin on a sharp piece of bent metal, then he scurried to the front, hoping to see them, to follow them.

There! They were only across the intersection, heading north on Henley. He tailed them another two blocks to the Downtown Hilton, where he dared not go farther at risk of being detected by not only Paul and Robin, but by others in the hotel. From the darkness of the sidewalk, he could see the bright lights of the lobby, and the concierge and the reception girls and the bellboys. Bellboys, especially, were to be avoided. Murphry knew them from their eyes; he'd always known about bellboys. They pretended to be just about the luggage and the tips, but they were secret employees of the False Government, hired to watch for secret employees of the True Government. Who would suspect a bellboy? Tidy little uniform, tidy little smile, tidy little mannerisms of respect and subservience. Tiny little vultures. Any time Murphry found himself on a street on which sat a nice hotel, and he was compelled to walk by, he saw the looks on their faces, the glances they gave each other. They had their suspicions about him, though it was clearly against their training to do more than watch. To look. To listen.

But today it didn't matter. He couldn't let Paul and Robin get away without gathering more information to save the hapless boss who would soon be separated from his head. Murphry gathered his courage and strode across the street and right into the hotel lobby past the slitty-eyed bellboys.

Immediately, a man in a uniform hastened over. "Sir, may I help you?"

He's security. He thinks I'm one of those crazy homeless people who try to get warm in the library or a hotel because they don't know any better.

"No. Thank you," said Murphry.

"I think perhaps you're lost?" pressed the security man.

"No, I'm with the convention."

"Oh? What convention is that?"

Murphry's eyes scanned the lobby and he spotted a poster on an easel near the elevators. He read aloud, "The Annual Meeting of Lycra-Spandex Professionals of America. I'm with that."

The security man scoffed as only a security man can, his reddened cheeks puffing and his fat nose twitching. He said, "I don't think so, sir. Let me help you. I'm sure you can find what you're looking for outside."

Fool! You have no idea what I'm looking for! But Murphry didn't want to draw any more attention to himself because that would not only ruin this case but future cases. He let the security man walk him to the front door and with a hefty shove, move him out.

The bellboys laughed aloud.

Back on the other side of the street, Murphry chastised himself. He wasn't prepared, and there he went, making a mess of things.

It's because you aren't letting the words lead the way.

Yes. True. He'd been rash. He had until tomorrow. He should never let passion, fear, or anger dictate his actions. Even with Kate, he was able to hold things in check. He needed to sit down. He needed a place with lighting.

The sky opened up and dumped a sudden, heavy rain onto the city.

He needed a place that was dry.

The library was closed, of course, as it was well after midnight. And the shelter was always full come midnight. If he and Kate were allowed to actually be together privately, he'd go to her place this moment, slip into her apartment through the window so as not to alert the neighbors, crawl into her bed next to her, and use her bedside lamp to do his work. He was sure she had a bedside lamp. Ladies like Kate were readers, and lady readers always had bedside lamps. Probably one shaped like a fairy or a tulip or a unicorn. But he and Kate were not allowed, so Murphry went to the closest convenience store/gas station instead. He stood in the middle of the gas pump island in the flickering lights with a couple brown paper towels from the dispenser pressed against a gas pump. He let his gaze travel across every sign and piece of printed matter within sight, and let the words tell him which ones to copy onto the paper towel "Kool gives you taste worth waiting for!" "Free 24 oz. soft drink of your choice with purchase of any 12-pack Yummy Cakes doughnuts." "Pay First Pump After." "This Pump Does Not Work." "Lotto Tickets on Sale Inside." "Southern Chewing Tobacco—Take Our Word For It!"

A car horn honked right behind him, causing him to flinch and toss the pen onto the gravel. He snatched it up and moved out of the way of the driver, who cursed him from behind his rolled up window glass. Murphry sat on a curb next to the restrooms under the lip of the roof. Drips splashed on his feet. On an increasingly-damp paper towel, he wrote his clues down, filling in the blanks with random words and punctuation that flashed into his eyes from the western novel, kept open beside him with his knee.

"Yummy Cake doughnuts cause a fevered passion. In a baby carriage is the taste worth waiting for. A southern silvered ocean on sale inside, lotto tickets with any purchase. Sweat-slicked biceps drip filth and chewing tobacco into a 24-oz soft drink. Take our word for it—pay first. Your choice."

Your choice.

My choice.

What does that mean? What is my choice?

Murphry slid back as far as he could against the rough brick of the building and studied the paper in his hands. A drunk came out of the men's room, looked down at

Murphry, coughed, and spit at his feet. Didn't matter. Murphry's shoes were soaking wet, anyway. He went to the Haven Street Bridge and found that his favorite spot for sleeping was already taken by a homeless man. So, he had to seek out a dry spot nearby under a thick bush. He tucked his notes inside his shirt, curled up on the dry dirt, set his mental alarm clock for 6:30 AM, and then went to sleep.

He woke as the sky was growing light in the east over the river. The rain had stopped. His shoes were still wet but that didn't matter at the moment. Shoes were shoes. Heads were heads. He stood up, ignored the grumbles of the homeless men and women nearby in various bushes and beneath rusting car hoods and piles of splintery timber, and took the paper towel from inside his shirt. The ink was faint, but he knew what it said. He had thought about the words before he drifted off, and had dreamed about the words as he slept.

A quick stop by the shelter gave him a chance to brush his teeth with a free toothbrush and squirt of paste. Then he combed his hair, straightened his jacket, and went to the nearest pay phone. His shoes squeaked but they would dry. He fished the coins he'd found last night from his pants pocket. There was enough money to make his call and have a couple nickels left over.

Your choice. It was his choice, what to do. For the first time, he was instructed to go on his gut. This time, he was to choose his actions on his own and not interpret the long, discombobulated phrases. Maybe the True Government thought that was being nice after all these years of service. To Murphry, it was very unsettling.

With a shaky index finger, he dialed directory assistance and asked to be connected to the front desk of the Henley Street Downtown Hilton Hotel. The phone rang two times and then went into a menu. Press 1 for reservations. Press 2 for directions. Press 3 for local weather. Or hold for the next available operator.

Your choice. You'll be fine. They know what they're doing, telling you this.

He held for the next available operator. The music on the line as he waited was something he'd heard a long time ago, an instrumental version of some sweet love song that made him feel a little nauseated. Then a click, and a woman. "Henley Street Downtown Hilton, how may I help you?"

"I have a message for Robin. She's with the Lycra-Spandex convention there in your hotel."

"I'm sorry, sir. I'll need a complete name before I can relay a message to one of our guests."

Murphry slammed the phone down. He had made the wrong choice! They told him to choose, and he chose to call. What a mistake that was!

Stepping out of the booth, he glanced up and down the sidewalk. Had someone been watching him make this blunder? Murphry hastened behind a huge Dumpster at the mouth of a nearby alley, took his jacket off, and placed it over his arm. Okay, at least now he was in disguise. He was different from the man who had made the call.

Take our word for it. Your choice.

Murphry paced up and down the block. Maybe it meant it was his choice to obey the True Government, not how to obey. Yes, that was it! He needed to get back on track with the message. He hurried back to the gas station/convenience store. He had just over an hour to get this done, or a man would be relieved of his head and the death would be on Murphry's own.

He had enough money to buy one Yummy Cake doughnut and one Lotto ticket from the convenience store. A sweet pastry, a ticket, and the right kid would do the trick. It was coming together in his head and Murphry felt relieved once more. The message was clear. He had a fevered passion to save the targeted boss. Yummy Cake doughnuts would do the trick. He needed a kid, someone not long out of a baby carriage.

In the convenience store there was a calendar on the wall. A quick flip through the pages to July revealed a beautiful silvery ocean, a couple palm trees, and seashells on the sand. This proved he was in the right place. *Snap, snap.* The puzzle pieces were coming together. On the counter beside the lotto tickets were tins of Southern Chewing Tobacco. A beefy-armed man near the magazine rack dumped a packet of sugar into his large, likely 24-oz, coffee. The trickles on the side of the cup looked like brown drools of sweat. His teeth were yellowed, a sure sign that he partook of the nasty tobacco sold at the register. *Snap, snap, snap.*

Murphry paid the dollar-eighty-two to the woman behind the counter. Back outside, he approached a boy of about twelve who was rummaging through the trash bin near the restrooms. Murphry pulled on a wide grin. It felt uncomfortable, but he held it.

"Hello, there."

The boy looked up and his eyes narrowed. "What do you want?"

"I have a favor to ask you."

"I have a cell phone in my pocket. I'll call my Mom if you don't leave me alone. Perv!"

He doesn't have a cell phone. He's a homeless boy, or at least a very poor boy. I've seen him and his mother off and on at the shelter on Fourth Avenue. He's bluffing.

"I have a doughnut." Murphry held out the little waxy white paper bag. "That's for you. I have a Lotto ticket. That's for the bellboy if he asks for some sort of pay. I have a note I need you to take into the Henley Hotel and tack onto a bulletin board in the lobby. That's all there is to it. Can you help me out?"

The boy eyed the white bag. "You poison that thing?"

Was his smile slipping? Why wasn't the boy trusting him?

"You know I didn't poison it," Murphry said, struggling to sound confident. "I just came out of the store. It's fresh and good. Smell?" He opened the bag and held it toward the boy. The boy leaned forward slightly and took a sniff.

Then the boy rubbed his mouth. "Well, what's the note all about?"

"I have a friend who's staying there. I want to surprise her. You want the doughnut? The hotel is close by. Just two blocks over."

The boy shrugged. "Fuck it, why not?"

Murphry cringed. How sad. A young boy, not long from the baby carriage, talking like a trash-mouth already, using words that would not serve him well in the long run. The two walked to the hotel, the boy lagging back several feet as if afraid Murphry would try to touch him.

Standing on the sidewalk across the street from the bright and bustling lobby, Murphry handed the boy an envelope with a simple note he'd penned inside. He'd picked up the envelope from a bank's ATM window; the note inside was composed on one of the many business cards he'd collected over time. This card was from one "Arnold D. Rooker, Renovations and Additions." There hadn't been a lot of room to write on the back of the card, but the message was short and to the point.

For the briefest second, Murphry hesitated when the boy held out his hand. What if the boy took the doughnut and Lotto ticket, trashed the note, and ran away? So he said, "If you do this right, I will buy you another doughnut later."

The boy's eyes brightened slightly. Then he said, "I'll do it, okay. Don't get your racing-striped shorts in a damn twist."

I don't wear racing stripes, thought Murphry. *I don't even like NASCAR.*

Murphry said, "Spit on your finger and rub the right side of your cheek. You've got a dirt streak. Tuck in your shirt and flatten your hair. You have to look like you might be staying at the hotel. You have to act like you belong there."

The boy growled but did what Murphry said. Then Murphry passed over the bag, note, and ticket. The boy darted through the traffic between cars and up to the hotel door. One bellboy gave him a sidelong glance, said something Murphry couldn't hear, and the boy held up the white bag and smiled. The bellboy turned away to an elderly couple with several wheeled suitcases, and the boy entered the hotel.

Yes!

Through the big glass window, Murphry watched as the boy strolled purposefully to the board boasting the gathering of the Lycra-Spandex Professionals, pulled out one of the corner pins on the poster, and pinned the note to the board. No one in the lobby noticed him or seemed to care. Kids were lucky that way unless they were screaming or dressed all in black with piercings in their eyebrows, noses, and lips. Murphry knew that when Robin came downstairs to attend her 9 AM meeting, she would see "ROBIN" printed in large, bold letters on the envelope. And if she didn't, one of her buddies, like Paul, would. She'd get the note.

She had to get the note.

The boy came back out the hotel door, but Murphry quickly entered the shoe store behind him and stood out of sight next to a display case featuring all sorts of pointy-toed high heels. Murphry didn't have any money to buy the boy another doughnut. At least not now. He hadn't lied. When he ran into the boy again at the shelter or on the street, and when he had another 60 cents, a doughnut there would be. The boy wormed his way across the street and stared up and down the walkway. Murphry turned and pretended to study one jeweled pair of shoes so the owner wouldn't kick him out. Murphry could read the boy's lips as he cussed and stomped, and then crammed the doughnut in his mouth and stormed off. The boy should consider himself lucky. The bellboy didn't require the Lotto ticket. Maybe the ticket would pay off. Then Murphry would be off the hook for the doughnut.

"Are you going to buy those?"

The voice was terse, and Murphry didn't need to turn around to see that the store owner was heading his way with a frown.

He stepped back outside.

Next to the Henley Hotel was a jewelry store. The large digital clock in the store's window read 8:24:05. 06. 07. 08. A bus drove by at that very moment, a large advertisement on the side boasting the glory of Carlton Broder's Fine Shampoos and Styling Gels. "You'll be glad you did!" the advertisement screamed.

I'll be glad I did! Murphry's heart skipped a happy beat. The True Government was cheering him along his way!

He had to get in place. She would be down in the lobby any minute. She did not strike Murphry as the type who would be late.

There was a large, wire-fenced, graveled lot at the back of the Henley Hotel. Along the top of the fencing were several thick, twisted strands of razor wire to discourage intruders and vandals. There were numerous steel Dumpsters ("We keep the city clean!" boasted the Dumpsters' motto, and Murphry knew that spoke for him, as well) in the lot, along with cars belonging to some of the employees as well as an aluminum trailer. There was a loading ramp that sat beneath several large steel doors, likely the loading area for bulk food deliveries for the restaurant. Murphry could not get into the lot; the gate was shut and locked with some sort of electronic device. But it didn't matter. Robin would search until she found him. She would be more than anxious to talk to him and to hear him out.

The note on the business card read, "I have your daughter, Hannah. Do not tell anyone or her life will be in peril. Come out the back of the hotel to the rear lot as soon as you get this note. There, I will tell you what you have to do. Remember. Mum is the word!"

Murphry didn't have any qualms writing that note. No, he'd never lie with his voice. Writing it down was like writing a play or a fiction story. If she thought it was real, that was her problem. It would be one of *words'* little jokes. He would allow them to play their joke on her. Little jokes were one of words' ways of helping you out when need be.

Murphry stood in the alleyway outside the wire fence, pressed against a light pole. Anyone looking up the alley from the street would assume he was just a hotel employee out having a cigarette break. But anyone inside the hotel's lot would not be able to see his face. That was the idea. Robin did not need to know who he was. No, it was more than that. She *could not* know who he was. All she needed was his message, delivered to her and her alone.

He waited, staring down the alley at the traffic on the street. Cars sped by. Busses rumbled past. Two boys on skateboards flew along the sidewalk, clickety-clacking across the seams in the concrete, shouting to each other that the other was a loser, a dork, an idiot, a queer. Illegal skateboarding. Murphry hoped that soon he would have an assignment to clean up that dangerous, juvenile behavior! A dog trotted down the alley to the telephone and lifted his leg to pee. Murphry growled the pup away.

How many minutes has it been now? He couldn't see the jewelry store clock. He didn't have a watch. *Ten minutes? Fifteen? Is it nine o'clock yet?*

Suddenly he had a flash of fear. *What if she doesn't find the note? What if it has fallen off the bulletin board and the janitor swept it away? What if one of the bellboys found it and he and his buddies are laughing behind their white gloves because they know they've thwarted something important?*

A red convertible whizzed past on the street, with the top down. Who wanted a top down in November? Another person who was making life terrible for the rest of the world. That driver would get sick in that car with that cold, damp air, and they would go to the hospital and they would, of course, use their health insurance and that would drive up the cost for everyone else who had health insurance. Sometimes, the ills of the world were almost too much to bear.

"Who wrote this note?" It was Robin. Murphry flinched. He expected her to be upset, but wasn't ready for the furor in her voice. He heard someone grab the wire fence and shake it. "Are you out there?"

"I'm here," Murphry said, reining in his fear.

"Behind the pole there! Look at me, you fucking coward!" Her voice was shrill and her breathing was heavy. "Explain what you mean in this note! Where is my baby?"

Murphry did not look around, of course. He stared down the alley at the busy street as he spoke. "You must not decapitate Mr. Clark. You must not assign anyone else that duty. Do you understand?"

"What?" The fence rattled harder. "What the fuck are you talking about?"

"I must have your promise. You will not separate Mr. Clark from his head. Do I have your assurance of that?"

"You fucking shit, where is Hannah?"

Banga-banga-banga went the wire fence. It sounded as if she was trying to tear it down.

"Where is Hannah?"

Murphry said, "She is safe. She is in a safe place." Murphry knew it was a fair assumption that the girl was in a safe place. Robin would not leave the girl in a place that was dangerous while she was off at a Lycra-spandex convention.

"I called my house," Robin said, "and no one answered. So either my nanny has taken Hannah out without carrying her cell, which I can't imagine her doing, or you're telling me the truth. Are you working for my ex? He's insane and always swore he'd have Hannah back! I'll kill you! I'll chop *your* damned head off!"

Me, too? First Clark, then me? This was much more unsettling than he'd imagined.

"I'll…" *banga-banga-rattle* "kill…" *rattle-rattle-rattle* "you if you don't tell me where she is! Right…now!" Her voice sounded higher. Not higher pitched, but higher up, like in the air above him. Murphry didn't glance around. Sound was being twisted to trick him into looking, like Lot's wife in the Bible. He remembered the pillar of salt story. Murphry didn't believe anyone had ever become a pillar of salt, but he knew that lack of self-control was a bad thing.

The rattling grew faster. *Rattle-rattle-rattle-rattle-rattle.* Robin was climbing the fence.

What if she got over? That wasn't supposed to happen! *She is supposed to be rational about this. All she has to do is promise not to kill Mr. Clark.* What was wrong with the woman?

She is the woman in black. No other would be this single-mindedly evil. She was pretending to be someone else, a subordinate of Clark's, to get in close enough to behead the man.

Murphry pulled his jacket up over his head to hide his face. He turned away from the light pole and rushed the fence. "Get down!" he yelled. "Get down now!" Robin was at the top, one leg over and the other swinging across. Murphry slammed into the fence with all his might. With a squall and a shriek, Robin wobbled, flailed, and dropped.

But not all the way.

Her head caught between two strands of razor wire. They snatched her up short by the neck. Her eyes went wide and white. Her legs kicked. Her hands flew to her neck and clawed at the offending noose. Murphry's jacket fell from his face and he stared at the woman as she struggled. The wire bit deeper and deeper into her neck. Streams of blood coursed down the front of her corporate jacket and over the little plastic-covered name tag pinned there on her left breast. She gurgled and hissed. For one fleeting moment, her gaze met Murphry's.

She's seen me now. The woman in black knows who I am. The horror of it gripped him by the throat. He couldn't breathe.

And then she stopped kicking. Her hands dropped to her side. Her tongue lolled.

There was a sharp sting in his lungs as his breathing resumed. *But I have succeeded in killing her before she killed me.*

Murphry backed away from the fence. He glanced up and down the alley. No one was there, watching. Murphry trotted back to the street, straightened his clothes, and strolled back into the city's persistent flow. He would throw away the shirt he'd worn while speaking with the doughnut boy, so the boy could never identify him in the future. Not that Murphry had killed the woman. Since she was in disguise, that's just what she was; a woman trying to save her daughter, no more. She had killed herself. *Maybe, people will think, she really did it because of the guilt she felt over the foul deed she had planned for Clark.*

He found the spoon in his pocket and began to rub. A cool calm coursed through his veins and his muscles. All was right again, at least for a moment. Passing the "Vintage Videos" store, he glanced at the various posters on the window glass. "The Wild Bunch." "Daring Dobermans." "Love Story." "Bird On a Wire."

Murphry stopped, stared, and nearly giggled. *What was to be a head on a platter,* Murphry thought, *turned into Robin, a bird on a wire.*

He smiled at that little play on words.

Words. A Secret Policeman's best friend.

Pulled the Wool Over His Eyes: Case #4

9:56 PM—Thursday, November 12th

D.D. MURPHRY, SECRET POLICEMAN, had hoped that word of his triumph over the woman in black would quickly reach Kate and that he would somehow be rewarded. But there was no indication that she'd heard about it. He told himself that this didn't mean anything and went on with his work.

Long ago Murphry had decided it was best to reduce any long term exposure to other individuals by rotating through the various homeless communities and shelters, spending no more than a month in each. Of course, when instructed to stay at a certain site, he did so.

This week he would become part of the Under Blunt crowd, as they were called. The Blunt street overpass created a perfect shelter for the homeless at the southern end of the rail yard. The Under Blunt crowd were twenty to thirty individuals who made their homes in the shelter of the overpass. They were generally quiet and respectful of Murphry's privacy and space—all but Blanche, a scrawny, ropy, chain-smoker in her late sixties. No matter how many times he told her he didn't smoke, she continued to ask, "Bum a butt?" every time she saw him.

The Under Blunt Crowd got along with one another fairly well because Big Serious, a giant of a man, veteran of the war in Afghanistan, kept the peace. When Big Serious was staying Under Blunt, those who were up to no good stayed away. Big Serious had made it *physically* clear that he tolerated no *tomfoolery,* even going to jail a time or two for using violence to defend the place and its inhabitants. He was powerful, fast and hyper vigilant. On one occasion he had frightened away a young thug who threatened to cut Murphry with a knife if he didn't give up his shoes. Murphry had thanked him, but Big Serious had merely turned around and walk away. He seemed to want nothing for his service but a little peace and quiet.

Trouble was he wasn't always around to keep the peace. Murphry'd heard he had a sister who took him in from time to time and found him work. Then his PTSD would flair up and he'd threaten someone and he'd be back out on the street again. Big Serious was really a very sad, paranoid, soft-hearted fellow. Murphry was pretty sure he liked him, but wasn't absolutely certain he wasn't False Government.

Big Serious was here tonight and the word was he expected to be here for some time to come, so Murphry felt safe.

And he liked it here. If the weather held, he could see himself staying for a week or so. It was a bit late in the season to be sleeping out under the stars, but Murphry had a new used sleeping bag from the recycling center and he was looking forward to being lulled to sleep by what he called the "whale song" of the rail yard. There was something satisfying about the deep, chunky sounds the engines and cars made, as they bunched and coupled, then strained to hold onto each other as they began to move as one unit. But it was the sound of the brakes which really spoke to him much the way he imagined Blues music spoke to others, a beautiful but lonely sound so similar to a recording he'd heard in the library of whales singing.

He hoped that when he and Kate were finally allowed to be together, that she might be so moved by these sounds that she would come here occasionally with him to camp out. Of course this would be done only when Big Serious was here to maintain order. That got him thinking that there was no real way for him to know if she would like the sounds of the rail yard. That led to anxiety with the realization that he didn't know if they had anything in common and that time was slipping away. He and Kate had been given no time to share with one another their cares, concerns, likes and dislikes. He pushed the anxiety back down with the promise that once Kate was finally and truly his, they would make up for the lost time.

Tonight ash can fires lit the underbelly of the overpass with orange light. The murmur of those clustered around the cans for warmth, and of course Blanche making the rounds asking everyone for a cigarette, blended pleasantly with the rail yard sounds. But the appearance of silhouettes and voices he didn't recognize marred the mood. One of the silhouettes, that of a woman seemed darker than shadow, blacker than black. When Blanche asked her for a cigarette, the woman ignored her.

Could it be?

No, there was no way. Murphry had killed her, hadn't he?

Perhaps I killed someone else.

Even if it were the woman in black, he was wearing a wool ski mask for warmth so there was no way she could identify him.

Wait a minute—does my disguise provide everyone with the means to trick me? Sure, I'm looking out through the holes right now, but if I fall asleep, someone could pull the wool over my eyes! Does that really make me more vulnerable?

He turned away from her and pulled the ski mask off his head. Just to be safe, he decided to put something between himself and the woman's silhouette. Without getting out of his sleeping bag, he inch-wormed around behind the nearby overpass support. Once she was out of view, he tried to let go of thoughts of the woman in black and trust that Big Serious would keep them all safe.

The graffiti on the concrete overhead, much of it so stylized as to be unreadable, appeared to writhe and flow across the surface in the flickering firelight. Occasionally, Murphry caught a brief message. The letter "W" had a lot of power tonight.

"Will the whole world away and worry goes with it."

He decided to take this advice and drifted off to sleep.

When he awoke in the morning everyone was gone but for Big Serious and a woman Murphry knew by the name of Rebecca Anne. Miss Anne was the only person Murphry was absolutely certain was a True Government employee. She and Big Serious were talking quietly as they sat on upturned milk crates beside a small fire pit. There was a pot of water about to boil on the fire. Big Serious poured the water into two cups that were standing ready with tea bags on another milk crate. Miss Anne and Big Serious seemed to be unaware that Murphry was awake. Perhaps they did not even know he was nearby. Perhaps she had come to recruit Big Serious. Murphry liked the thought of that, and it most certainly meant that Big Serious was not False Government.

Miss Anne raised her cup of tea, blew on it and took a sip as she consulted a small notebook resting on her knees. Then she said something to Big Serious that Murphry could not hear. Big Serious had a faraway look in his eye—*His thousand-yard-stare*, Murphry thought—then looked back at her with his eyes narrowed and slowly shook his head.

Yes, Murphry had also quickly become suspicious of her....

It was several years ago, shortly after Murphry had received the call to become a Secret Policeman, that Rebecca Anne had first approached him in the dining area of the Fourth Avenue homeless shelter. She was tall and thin, very blonde, and had a friendly, open face. She sat at the table where Murphry was seated and spoke with the local rural accent, asking about his comfort at the shelter. "Do you have enough to eat? Do you have a job?"

Murphry was so new to being a Secret Policeman, he was still somewhat trusting of others. He believed now that at the time his employer had kept him just enough in the dark about his work that he would not be so suspicious of others as to prevent him from making contact with Miss Anne. He wondered if she were one of his secret colleagues or just a friendly concerned citizen. He was willing to answer her questions up to a point. "Yes, I have plenty to eat. I have a job, but it is a secret job I can't tell you about."

For this statement, he got from her one raised eyebrow, but then she went on without hesitation. "Do you have family in the area?"

That gave him a shot of adrenaline, but he didn't know why. "Did someone send you to find me?" he asked as he pushed away from the table, got up and backed away.

"No," she said with her open and honest face. "I don't know your family."

Murphry didn't know his family either—not any more. What he *felt* was that they wanted to control him in some way.

She might be up to no good, but I can't really tell.

"If you're uncomfortable talking about that," Miss Anne said, "we can change the subject."

Murphry got up and left the room. When he came back later, she was gone.

It looked as if Big Serious was going to follow in Murphry's footsteps. The big man got up and walked away from Miss Anne, glancing back to make sure she was leaving the area. Miss Anne retreated back up the gravel slope toward the overpass and disappeared from sight.

Murphry approached Big Serious who was crouched with his back turned in a makeshift wood and tar paper structure loading a backpack. He immediately regretted this—everyone knew better than to sneak up on Big Serious. Murphry stood there unable to open his mouth to speak or move for fear the man might be startled and turn on him with a knife or a gun. He had a sudden need to urinate and wondered if he'd have to do it just standing there.

Finally Big Serious said, "What do you want to say, Mr. Quiet? It must be real important 'cause I never seen you say nothing to no one."

Murphry could feel himself constricting his urethra to save himself from embarrassment. "She can help you out," he said in a voice he thought was perhaps so quiet it would not be heard.

"Yes, but then she would want something from me."

The big man shouldered the backpack and trotted up the gravel slope and out of sight.

A few days later Murphry awoke again to see Miss Anne talking with Big Serious. The big man was shaking his head again. Murphry wanted to step in and set his mind at ease—*Big Serious would make a great and powerful Secret Policeman*—but he decided he should stay out of it. He got up and walked to the portable toilet the city had installed for the Under Blunt Crowd. When Miss Anne saw him she gave him a little wave. He waved back.

The second time Murphry had met her was about a week after their first meeting. It also took place in the kitchen of the Fourth Street Shelter.

"Hello, Mr. Murphry. Do you remember me?"

"Yes, I remember you," Murphry said, thinking belligerent thoughts but speaking with a soft and even voice, "and your notebook and that little black box on your belt with the red flashing light. Yes, I remember things."

"Can I sit with you for a minute?"

"Suit yourself."

"I feel like we got off to a bad start last time and I'm sorry if I made you feel uncomfortable."

"I just don't understand why you want to know about my family."

"I asked you that because I wonder if you have any support here in the city? You know, anyone you can go to if you need something."

"I can take care of myself." Murphy said, doing his best to maintain his composure. "I have a job."

Miss Anne turned her eyes away, wrote something in her notebook.

"What are you writing?" he asked, trying but failing to keep the strain out of his voice, "and why won't that light stop flashing on your belt?"

"I wrote that you said you had a job to help me remember it."

"Why do you need to remember it? What business...?" He let his voice trail away.

Miss Anne put the notebook away and turned her calm blue eyes on him with no raised eyebrows. "Sometimes I forget things and I get really frustrated with that. So I take notes to help me remember. The red light tells me that my pager is turned on. The pager helps me stay in touch with the people I work for when I'm out of the office."

"Is someone listening to us through that right now?"

"No, it's not a phone. It just alerts me if someone is trying to call me on the telephone, but I can turn it off." She reached down with a finger and pushed something on the black box and the light went out. "How do you stay in touch when you're away from your work?"

She either knows something and is with me or she's trying to trick me into giving her something she can use against me.

Again, Murphry was so new to being a Secret Policeman that he had only the most vague notions of the enemy he would be fighting. His suspicious nature and intuition— traits that would later become invaluable to his work—were not well-developed.

If she is evil, maybe she wants to take my job away? Being as yet unaware of how special his relationship with words was, he couldn't think of anything else that he had that she might find valuable. She might take his life, but then he hadn't succeeded in doing anything much that might have made that worth taking. He had yet to solve any cases at all.

He was uncomfortable enough to want to get up and leave, but his desire to be recognized and acknowledged by a colleague kept him in his seat.

Murphry shrugged in answer to her question.

"Let me tell you a little about myself," Miss Anne said. "I grew up on a farm about fifty miles from here. We had chickens, cows, rabbits and dogs and I spent most of my free time with them because I was shy as a child. As an adult, I want to help people out—it's my job—but sometimes I'm not very good at it because I am much better with animals than I am with people. If I am not communicating well with you maybe that's why and I apologize. Perhaps you could help me by letting me know if I am being clear or if I have made some sort of social blunder."

Murphry could understand being shy. There had been plenty of times in his life when his shyness had prevented him from being who he wanted to be. Miss Rebecca Anne seemed like a nice lady. She was pretty too. He nodded his head to show her he understood and he gave her a slight smile.

"I am a social worker," Miss Anne said. "I visit people, *like you*, in shelters to determine what resources they are lacking and try to help them to get what they need."

Like you meant to Murphry that she was singling him out, that she considered him special in some way. His suspicion that she was a secret colleague was stronger than ever, but he knew better than to ask her because you never knew when someone might be listening.

"The notes I take help me remember what their needs are," Miss Anne continued, "so I can determine what can be provided for them."

"Who provides?"

"If you qualify, the government will provide you with funds to help you get along in the world."

"*Qualify* has several definitions. One is that it means *to give authority to*. Is that the way you're using it?"

"Yes," Miss Anne said.

She's trying to help determine how much I'll get paid to work as a Secret Policeman. I'll get a pay check! "I already have the authority from the government."

"If that's *true* there should be no problem."

When she says true, *that implies that there is a* false. *A false what? If she has the power to determine how much money I get, then she must work for the government, but if they think I need it, why don't they just send me a paycheck already? Why this run-around? Is she trying to determine if I am* true *to the government I work for?*

Is my loyalty in question? Who would I sell that loyalty to—perhaps the implied *false, a* False Government?

Yes!—Murphry had seen evidence of that on the street, brutality from the police, a fire department that burned down houses, emergency responders who rounded up injured individuals, restrained them, and with their vehicles screaming to cover the cries of their captive, carted them away to who knew what hellish fate. But why? Was it just a power struggle between a False Government and the one Murphry worked for? Was that part of the reason he was a Secret Policeman?

"I *do* qualify," Murphry stated proudly—thinking, *I work for the* True Government—but knowing better than to say it out loud. " I *have* the authority, but… you need…proof, right?"

"Yes, well…I have a few more questions to ask. Do you mind if I take notes to help me remember?"

"That would be fine," Murphry said, offering her another small smile.

Most of the questions involved his current situation and needs and were not of a personal nature. Even so, Murphry took the precaution of answering them in a guarded manner. He did this in case anyone overheard.

"Now, has anyone ever told you about Social Security Income and Insurance that you may qualify for?"

Murphry remembered her as saying this a bit louder than necessary, perhaps so others could hear her. He had heard of Social Security before, but that was for old folks and disabled persons. *Of course…they would have a cover for their payroll—* you couldn't just pay a Secret Policeman openly. Murphry played dumb as he knew she wanted him to. After she finished explaining, she said he'd have to meet with someone else in order to get the ball rolling officially. At this point, he felt sure he could trust her.

When Murphry emerged from the toilet, Big Serious was speaking with his voice raised. "I'm not going to see no doctor. I know that's what you want and I'm not going to do it. I think you'd best stay away from here from now on."

He doesn't understand. He's too afraid.

Again Big Serious got up and walked away from Miss Anne. She collected her things and climbed the embankment. Blanche caught up with her at the top and said something to her Murphry couldn't hear, no doubt asking for a cigarette. Miss Anne shook her head and walked away out of sight.

Blanche continued down the slope toward Murphry.

Thinking about the situation with Big Serious, Murphry shook his head.

"I didn't even ask you yet," Blanche said as she approached.

It took Murphry a moment to realize she thought he was shaking his head at her. What he'd like to do was to shake some sense into Big Serious. He knew he could never do that. Murphry sympathized with the man because he too had been frightened, but was glad that the fear hadn't stopped him from meeting with Roderick. He wished he could tell Big Serious about his experience.

Murphry was sweating even though the room was nice and cool. *I must trust Dr. Roderick*, he repeated to himself for the thirty-second time as he listened to the next question and tried to come up with an honest answer. He trusted Miss Anne and she had brought him in to see the man. She was seated next to Murphry and occasionally gave him a reassuring smile.

Murphry had decided that Roderick was a Ph.D. rather than an M.D. because he had yet to strike his knee with a rubber hammer or press on his tongue with a popsicle stick. It made sense that the government would have highly intelligent, accomplished people in charge. *Of course it could be that he is playing the roll of a doctor to make this seem to outsiders like a simple visit to the doctor. That's pretty clever*, Murphry thought. He could play along with that.

Roderick, tall and with a protruding gut, sat behind a desk cluttered with framed photographs and littered with paper. His hands were folded over his little pot belly as he leaned back in his chair, sighting along the double barrel of his long, slim, shotgun-of-a-nose to keep Murphry in view. Murphry wished Roderick would clip the tangle of gray nose hairs that seemed to block each nostril for fear that if the man sneezed his face might explode.

Questions like "What is today's date? Where are we? Who is the president of the

United States currently?" had really obvious answers, but Murphry didn't make a big deal out of it.

"What does it mean," Roderick asked, "when someone says, *People who live in glass houses should not throw stones?*"

"It means they might break their house," Murphry said.

Roderick seemed preoccupied, as if his meeting with Murphry and Miss Anne should take only a small part of his brain power and attention, the rest being reserved for more important mental activities. Whatever he was doing with that brain power was not obvious. Murphry imagined him working on quantum physics equations in the intervals when Murphry was expected to deliver his answers to the seemingly endless questions. Even though he didn't seem to take any notice at all of Murphry's answers, every once in a while, he would ask Murphry to elaborate on one.

The questions were about age, medical history, marital status, sexual orientation, religious affiliation, education, work history, ability to hold down a job, his current situation concerning food, shelter and occupation.

In response to this last, Murphry said, "You already know about my job."

"Do I?" Roderick asked.

"Yes, of course, you know I can't speak about it out loud."

"Can you at least tell me about your duties?"

"Well, I can say that I fulfill my duties as I become aware of them. I would never fall down on the job. It means that much to me."

"And how is it that you become aware of your duties?"

"Is that a trick question? I'm certain you keep records of all our communication?"

"Have you been receiving communications from us regularly?"

"Why, yes, certainly."

"What would you say is our most common means of communicating with you."

"Through the newspaper—ads, movie reviews, sometimes in a comic," and Murphry chuckled remembering a particularly funny one despite his nervousness. He was immediately embarrassed and looked down at his lap as he said, "I try to get the paper every day," then he swallowed hard and looked back up at the man.

"I see," Roderick said and nodded his head sagely. He continued, asking Murphry where he had grown up, about his childhood experiences and his family. Did he have any siblings, any history of sexual/physical/emotional abuse. Were there traumatic experiences in his childhood. "Did you have problems in school?"

Murphry couldn't find many answers for most of these questions and they made him intensely uncomfortable. He felt his ears burning and wondered if one of his family were talking about him at that moment. He looked back down at his lap.

"Has anyone in your family had any mental illness or problems with substance abuse or dependence?"

Murphry didn't respond. He knew he must, but there was nothing there. He was relieved when Miss Anne explained to Roderick that Murphry's memory about his past, particularly his childhood, was incomplete. Roderick seemed irritated that she had spoken up and Murphry decided that he might have to trust the man, but he didn't have to like him.

"Have you ever undergone any medical treatment or surgeries, seen a psychiatrist, been hospitalized or attended outpatient therapy with a counsellor? Are you on any medication?"

Murphry explained that he had no such history, that he wasn't taking any drugs, and that as far as he knew, he was healthy.

"Have you had suicidal or homicidal thoughts," Roderick asked.

Since Murphry had never wanted to kill himself or harmed anyone without having been instructed to do so, the answer was, "No."

"Do you drink alcohol or use drugs."

"No."

"Can you tell me why you think Miss Anne has brought you to see me?" Roderick asked.

"Something to do with getting paid."

"Of course, the Social Security…But are you under any particular stress? Are you having any difficulties related to mood, thought process, functioning in your daily life, anything that is hampering your ability to provide for your own needs, such as depression, anxiety, fear, paranoia, hallucinations, delusions?"

The questions weren't threatening in and of themselves, but Murphry was definitely feeling threatened. There was a nauseating flutter deep in his gut that made him squirm in his seat. He knew that this was important. They were evaluating him to determine his worth in order to set his salary. If for no other reason than security, they would need to know all about him and perhaps he was also expected to play along with the ruse a bit, offer some suggestion as to why he would be coming to see a doctor. He reached for something he considered outrageous, something he'd heard another homeless man say. Locking his feet around each other and grabbing the arms of the chair, he forced himself to become still and then looked the man in the eye.

"I hear Mother Teresa's voice in my head..., telling me that even though I wasn't born yet, both World Wars are my fault and my punishment…is to be homeless and forgotten. There's…nothing I can do about it."

There was a long pause in which Roderick seemed to consider a picture hanging on the wall. Murphry worried the man had heard that one before and that somehow it wasn't good enough, but then the man turned to him and extended his hand.

"Thank you for coming in. I will give my written evaluation to Miss Anne and she will turn it in to Social Security with your application and we'll see what happens. In the mean time, let me give you this prescription..." He paused to scribble a note and handed it to Murphry. "...for some free medication you can pick up at the clinic. Miss Anne will tell you how."

Roderick showed them the door and they left the office. Murphry took a deep breath and let it out, feeling the tension drain from his limbs.

"It will probably be three to five weeks before we'll know if you qualify. Would you check back with me on a weekly basis until we find out?

"Yes, of course."

As Murphry left the building, he considered the note Roderick had given him. The scribble was almost impossible to make out, but finally he read, "Drop this in the nearest trash receptacle."

Of course, the prescription is part of the ruse.

Murphry had started receiving his pay check a few weeks later and had received it regularly ever since. He met with Miss Anne every month for over a year. She asked if he were taking his medications and he would tell her that he was because he knew that was what she wanted him to say. The truth was that even though he went to the clinic to get the medications every month, he did not take them. He stored them in his locker at the bus station.

Over time their meetings changed; her questions seemed to indicate some suspicion. She wanted to know more about what he did as a Secret Policeman, but Murphry's methods were his own and for security reasons he would not divulge them to anyone. "It all has to do with parking meters and is very boring," he told her several times. If she wanted the basic facts of the cases he solved, she surely had access to files that could inform her. Maybe her job was boring and she just wanted to get in on the excitement of his work vicariously, but at their last meeting, he wondered briefly if she had gone over to the other side. Then she had smiled and he had dismissed the notion that she would have anything to do with the enemy, the False Government.

Then he had become really busy and couldn't make their meetings. He hadn't spoken to her in over a year when he saw her on the street about a week ago. She startled him as she came around a corner at Third and McKinley. At first glance Murphry thought she was the woman in black, back from the dead. He was ready to take off running when he realized his mistake. What about her had impressed him that way? She wasn't even wearing black, but something about her gave that distinct impression. Then she smiled and it went away.

"I'm sorry—I didn't mean to startle you Mr. Murphry."

Murphry shrugged as if to say it was no big deal, but the adrenaline in his system made him want to hop up and down just to stay put. He did his best to remain still and maintain his dignity.

"We haven't met in a long time. Would you make an appointment with my office to come in soon?"

"I will."

"My cousin is visiting and somehow we got around to talking about you. She said you sounded interesting and that she'd like to meet you. Perhaps when you come in for your appointment?"

What is Miss Anne doing talking to people about me? Her cousin at one of our appointments? Perhaps she is one of us.

Again Murphry shrugged.

"Please call my office."

"Okay," he said, but knew he had no intention of doing so.

It was in the following week that she started coming to see Big Serious.

The day after Big Serious's harsh words to Miss Anne, Murphry was headed across the Blunt Street overpass when he heard Blanche shouting from the other side. "Mr. Henry!" There was an unusual desperation about her, as she waved her hand and ran toward him. *She must really need one,* Murphry thought. When she was only a few yards away she stopped to catch her wheezing breath and say, "It's Big Serious, Mr. Henry. He's gone crazy again and this time he's pulled a knife on that nice lady, Miss Anne, what comes to visit Under Blunt." She gestured for him to follow as she turned back the way she'd come. Murphry hurried after her.

"She come to talk to that new guy, you know, Mr. Lowell Brownlee?" She coughed out the words as she ran. "When Big Serious saw her, he tol' her she wasn't welcome there anymore. She said she had every right to talk to people Under Blunt. That's when he pulled the knife. She left and now he's holed up in that tar paper box o' his. Won't come out."

As they proceeded down the gravel embankment, Murphry told her there wasn't anything he could do about it. "Besides, it seems like the situation is over. She left like he wanted her to."

There were ten or fifteen of the Under Blunt crowd beneath the overpass. They were clearly upset by the turn of events as they clustered around the bridge supports.

"Yeah, but what if she returns?"

"She won't."

Just as he said this two police cars came to a stop with their grills just visible at the top of the embankment. Four policemen and Miss Rebecca Anne got out.

What is she doing? Murphry thought.

Miss Anne stood at the top and pointed toward the tar papered box.

No! What is she doing with the False government? What do they know? What has she told them?

The officers pulled their weapons and began to descended.

If she needed help, she should have asked me. As soon as he thought this he had a twinge of shame, realizing that he would have been afraid to deal with Big Serious. He was glad he wasn't here when the conflict started.

That was it! I wasn't available. It seemed like a good reason, a reasonable excuse, but it raised a lot of other questions that he tried unsuccessfully to ignore. He didn't want to think she'd call on the enemy for help unless there was no other course available.

No, she knows what she's doing. I just don't have all the facts.

As the officers moved around Under Blunt, the inhabitants, including Murphry, found cover wherever possible. When the policemen were fifty feet from the tar papered box they spread out and surrounded it, aiming their weapons stiffly.

"Lawrence Mayfield," One of the officers shouted, "It's officer Manley. Looks like it's that time again. Are you ready for another nice sit down talk and a warm meal?"

Although the officer gave a long pause, there was no answer, but muffled curses came from within the box.

"You can't just go around scaring folks like this. Now, I want you to throw your knife out and then come on out of that box?"

More cursing came from the box until it was drowned out by pounding on the inside walls. The box rocked back and forth and one wall split open a little. The police backed away, all but Officer Manley, and the Under Blunt Crowd ducked down and scurried for better cover. Murphry could see Big Serious's eye peeking out through the crack.

"We know you don't want to hurt anyone," Manley continued. "You don't have to pretend for us. We know you very well by now."

There was another long pause and finally Big Serious spoke. "What you serving down to the Jail tonight?

"I think it's grilled cheese, hog rotten potatoes and three bean salad."

"I like that three bean. You give me an extra helping?"

"I'll see to it personally."

The curtain of tar paper at the entrance parted enough for the knife to be tossed out into the dirt. Officer Manley walked over and retrieved it then bent down to offer Big Serious a hand and help him up out of the box. The big man was handcuffed and escorted to one of the police cars and they drove away. Miss Anne went with them.

In the days that followed, Murphry thought he'd successfully justified Miss Anne's involvement with the False Government, but it was increasingly difficult to ignore the questions. They began to gnaw at him at night when he was trying to sleep and distract him in the daytime when he was trying to assemble text into meaningful communication.

Why had she been in such a hurry to deal with Big Serious that she had involved the False Government? How had she explained to them her involvement with the big man? What had she divulged to Big Serious in trying to recruit him that he might have revealed in a police interview?

Murphry liked Miss Anne and didn't want to think the unthinkable. He hoped and looked for messages from his employer that would give him all the facts, but found none. Then he saw the headlines on a newspaper in a dispenser on the street—Near-*Miss* for Earth/Asteroid—If Sus*anne* Kulp *is* Elected!—State Department *Traitor* Unveiled.

He received the message loud and clear—Miss Rebecca Anne would have to be taken out. A dread set in and he couldn't pull himself together to get any work done for the rest of the day. His relationship with Miss Anne was the longest association he could remember clearly. He had liked and trusted her. She was pretty too.

Even so, he began to come up with a plan. He would make a cocktail from all the medication he'd been storing in his locker and somehow get her to drink it. He knew from his reading about the medicine that it would not kill her, but she would be highly sedated. This would give him a chance to lay her out on the railroad tracks in front of an oncoming train.

He checked the rail yard schedule online to determine the best time to meet with her, then called to make that appointment she had requested and asked her to meet with him Under Blunt. She agreed to meet him there the next day.

As the appointment neared, he spread the rumor that the Tritop Bakery on Front Street was dumping a days worth of baked goods because of a health risk. All of the Under Blunt Crowd hurried off to the bakery. Then Murphry sat to boil water at the fire pit and prepare the medicated tea he would serve Miss Anne. He went over in his head his plans for dragging her to the tracks and promised himself he would not look when the train struck her. Even so, the images rolled through his head, limbs flying and blood spewing.

Then she was late and he began to fear he might lose his opportunity. The Under Blunt Crowd would soon realize the truth and return. Some might be angry.

Time passed and the trains he'd meant to do the job for him came and went. The under Blunt Crowd came straggling back giving him dirty looks.

Blanche appeared at the top of the embankment, cigarette poking from her mouth, and tried to run down the slope toward Murphry. She tripped and fell face-forward down the gravel slope. Murphry hurried to help her and when he got there she was still lying there holding her skinned arms and sides and moaning. There was a gash on her chin, but the lit cigarette, bent but not broken, still protruded from her mouth. She took a puff as he lifted her to her feet.

"Miss Anne," she said, tears in her eyes. "I saw her car crash through the barrier and fall into the Charter Canal. It sank and took Miss Anne and her passenger with it. They saved the passenger—she's all right—but they been trying to get Miss Anne out for the last half hour. I think she's gone Mr. Henry."

"Was the passenger her cousin?" Murphry asked.

"I never seen her before—a woman all dressed in black."

Murphry sat down in the gravel. None of it made any sense at first, but then he began to see the sense in it and was relieved. A great weight had been lifted and was replaced by a sadness.

The woman in black is back. Did she manipulate Miss Anne or even blackmail her?

Blanche sat next to him, blood drooling down her forearms and chin. "I'm sorry, Mr. Henry. She was a nice lady."

"Yes, she was," Murphry said.

They took pity on me and had someone rig her brakes or something. Too bad they didn't get the woman in Black.

I hope they don't see me as weak.

Under My Skin: Case #5

10:35 AM—Friday, November 31st

D.D. Murphry, Secret Policeman, savored the small cup of grape juice he'd been given after uploading his fresh personality traits to his superiors. He noticed that a drop had escaped and dripped off his chin onto the Sunday paper in his lap.

"Drink that slowly and relax for a moment before leaving the building," the nurse told him.

They always told him that. They told everyone that. *Whether you're here on business for the True Government or come in off the street to sell blood for some extra cash,* Murphry thought, *everyone is treated the same, so no one becomes suspicious. And certainly no one questions the need for blood.* He chuckled inwardly. *As if anyone should ever have to pay for blood when more blood is spilled daily in the fight against crime than could ever be used.*

His eyes lit upon the grape juice spot, once bright purple-pink, now turning blue on the newspaper in his lap. The droplet had landed next to the words, "quite ingenious."

Yes, he agreed, it was all quite ingenious, how the public had been convinced to give blood, how unknowingly those who did were providing their personality profiles to the True Government, how offering payment for blood had attracted those the True Government most wanted to keep tabs on—the ne'er-do-wells, the poor and desperate, those who wanted something for nothing—in short, those most likely to engage in criminal behavior. Murphry should know—he had once been among them.

But he wasn't afraid for the True Government to have his blood. He had nothing to hide. Well, perhaps some sexual fantasies about his beloved Kate and his frustration over not consummating their marriage, but nothing he was really ashamed of. Certainly nothing criminal. Having his fresh personality allowed his employer to fine-tune their communication. And, of course, the process of "buying" his blood allowed them to put a little extra money in his pocket.

Murphry made a game of determining who was here on business for the agencies that employed him and who wasn't. Some of the men and women he saw today he knew from the local streets. There were plenty who were genuinely insane, but he was certain there were far fewer than most people suspected.

The old woman across the room for example—she was wearing four different colored hair pieces, she was knitting the air in front of her with wild gestures and ranting loudly about, "The candle, the candle—don't let it blow out." It was easy to believe that she was mentally ill because she was drawing attention to herself with her appearance and odd behavior. But then everyone but Murphry was trying to ignore her, which meant her actions might have been carefully planned and executed to provide cover.

Not knowing the truth about such things used to bother Murphry, but now that he was part of the well-oiled machinery of the True Government, such questions had become the stuff of fun and games, not to be taken too seriously. He knew better than to talk to anyone about it, even those he suspected of being his secret colleagues. He was not willing to risk blowing his cover for something as trivial as satisfying his curiosity.

Murphry looked at the newspaper and gathered the third word from the third line in each of the paragraphs in the third column of the page open on his lap. He had to add a "the" and an "in" of his own and borrow the word "among" from one of the headlines to make a complete sentence. Their communications would be smoother and more complete once they had had time to process his fresh personality traits, but it was plain what his superiors were trying to say to him: "They hide in plain sight among the general public."

Yes, there were those who Murphry couldn't place in the "Seriously Disturbed" or "Secret True Government Employee" categories. These formed two additional categories: "False Government Employees" and "The General Public." The latter were the group from which most common, unaffiliated criminals emerged.

Murphry always kept a wary eye on those of "The General Public" whom he saw at the Blood Bank. The two fellows sitting next to him were of this group. They seemed harmless, however, talking about personal matters, their voices almost at a whisper. Murphry, having trained himself to tightly focus his listening, heard everything they said. Their current conversation was an inane one about the problems the tall blonde fellow was having with his girlfriend. Having finished their juice, they were getting up to leave when the tall one said to his rotund companion, "I don't know, man.... She gets so angry with me. Last night I was five minutes late and she jumped down my throat."

Could this be a crime? Murphry wondered. There seemed to be a rash of cannibalism in the city of late. Just yesterday he heard a woman say to a man, "We'd love to have you for dinner." To Murphry's horror, the man accepted. Then they parted company and Murphry didn't know whom to follow. One was soliciting cannibalism; the other was willing to facilitate it. He let them both go as he had other pressing business.

The girlfriend jumping down her boyfriend's throat seems a case of forced cannibalism. But what's the point? Is she inside him to take control of his body and mind? If she can get her blood into his, it might work.

"I don't know what to say to you," the fat one said, "I never liked the skinny bitch to begin with."

She would have to be very skinny indeed, wouldn't she?

Murphry would follow the poor fellow with the girlfriend inside him and see what he might do to help. The man's bearing and the way he spoke about it made it obvious he was embarrassed by the whole thing—if he'd been able to get her out on his own, he would have.

Outside the blood bank the two companions said goodbye to one another and walked in opposite directions. Murphry followed at a distance as the guy with his girlfriend inside walked to the parking lot, got into a pickup truck and drove away.

Damn! That's the fourth time this week I've lost someone.

Murphry was ashamed of himself for cursing, even inside his own head. He remembered his religious aunt Martha, his father's sister, who wanted to "double damn" things all the time, but was unwilling to utter the word "Damn." Instead she'd just say, "D D this" and "D D that." When he was very young, he'd thought she was referring to him in her anger and it frightened him terribly. Now, even though he wasn't religious, he believed that cursing showed poor character.

He'd been hoping to acquire a vehicle for some time now, but his employer obviously hadn't yet seen the necessity of that.

In his frustration, he rummaged through the loose packages of lollipops in his jacket pocket until he found his spoon stress-reliever. Although the eating utensil normally remained in his pocket while he rubbed it, he pulled it out to see the blood stain in the concave business end. It was almost completely worn off.

Murphry had a sudden fear that by rubbing the stain, he had somehow caused the blood to get inside him. *No*, he told himself, *my calluses are too thick. Just make sure you don't rub it if you cut your thumb.*

Tinged with fear, his frustration was slow to recede. It escalated into thoughts of failure and Kate ultimately rejecting him.

Murphry took a deep breath. *All I can do is take things as they come, he reminded himself. Back to collecting aluminum cans for the True Government.*

Murphry located the big black garbage bag he'd hidden in the bushes out front of the blood bank. He shook it to get an idea how many cans were in it, then moved off in search of more. It was a tedious job he did in his spare time. The True Government could get at least a partial personality profile off the lip of each can, and he was paid to collect them—one more way his employer could put a little money in his pocket.

An hour later, Murphry was in Franklin Park going through trash receptacles when he cut his thumb on a jagged soda can. While he was distracted, a man wearing six sweaters and three hats ran off with his bag of cans.

Murphry rubbed the thumb into his spoon to soothe the pain and his frustration. When he realized what he was doing he cried out and flung the spoon away. It landed on the pavement in an intersection of sidewalk just as a woman on a red scooter came tearing through making a turn, her dreadlocks flapping in the wind. Her front wheel hit the spoon and the scooter slipped out from under her. She hit the plinth of a monument hard with her head and went down. Her scooter came to rest in the bushes next to the monument. It was still running.

Murphry looked to see if anyone was watching, but saw no one. "Serves you right," he said to the unconscious woman. "It is clearly posted that these walkways are for non-motorized traffic only."

Murphry looked for his spoon, but saw it had fallen into a drain. He knew he couldn't get his fingers through the drain cover and would have to abandon it. He turned and looked the scooter over. It seemed none the worse for wear. He'd been needing something like this. Now he'd be able to give chase in traffic if need be. There was a chain and lock with its key still in it wrapped around the rack on the back so he'd be able to secure it wherever he went. He placed a "thank you" in his mind where he was sure his employer would find it next time he gave blood, then righted the vehicle, climbed on, put it in gear and rode out of the park.

It was Monday morning when Murphry was awakened by a voice. "I don't know, man…. She got under my skin and now I can't be without her."

It sounded to Murphry like the guy with the girlfriend inside him. He had been awakened from a nightmare in which someone had gotten into his blood stream, had taken control of his body and was forcing him to eat his own hands. They tasted okay, but caused him to feel nauseated.

Murphry pushed the dream out of his mind and sat up. He had slept in his clothes again. This "camping out" was getting tiresome. He had been instructed to stay here, but didn't know why. *It could be worse,* he reminded himself. *At least the weather has continued to be relatively warm.* He'd been looking for the messages instructing him to start sleeping somewhere else, but had not seen one. The beds were softer at the mission.

Murphry crawled out of his sleeping alcove under the Haven Street bridge and looked up to see who was speaking. Against the bright morning sun, he saw the silhouettes of two men who appeared to be fishing off the bridge. Neither silhouette looked like the tall blonde fellow he'd seen at the blood bank, but then people changed from situation to situation, didn't they? He thought he'd seen these guys fishing here every weekend for the past three weeks he'd been staying here, but hadn't taken much interest in them. This was no doubt why he didn't recognize the blonde fellow at the blood bank yesterday.

"I know I should just leave," the man said, "but I can't get her out of my head."

If she's under his skin and inside his head, it sounds like she got her blood into his. He remembered thinking of this possibility outside the blood bank. *Did she take that thought from my head?* Murphry certainly hoped she had not. He hated to think that he had caused this fellow additional pain because he wasn't maintaining good thought discipline. What would Kate think of him if she found out? *Perhaps I should hide the thought in one of the deepest folds of my brain,* he thought, but realized he didn't really know how to go about doing that.

Murphry went back to his alcove and retrieved his fishing supplies, an abbreviated rod with a kite string reel on it and some rancid bacon. He then climbed to the top of the bridge on the side opposite the two fishermen. Waiting for a car to pass, he set his bait, then he crossed to the other side of the bridge and stood at the railing about twenty feet downwind of the other fisherman and cast his line.

The fishermen were engrossed in their conversation and paid him no mind.

"She's sleeping with some guy," the blonde one said. Murphry noticed that his nose was a lot longer than it had been yesterday at the blood bank. Also, his hair had begun to recede, he was much more muscular and well-built and he wasn't nearly as tall. It seemed she had altered his appearance.

If she's inside him, but having sex with some other guy, then she's forcing him to have homosexual sex. Depending on how he feels about that, it could be real hell.

"What are you going to do about it?" his companion said. The guy had obviously dyed his hair red and lost a lot of weight. Murphry wasn't certain but it seemed he might also be wearing a mask to change his appearance.

"I don't know. We had a big argument about it. She wasn't willing to admit anything. Finally, I just threw up my hands and walked out."

My dream—I was this guy. She was making me eat my hands. And the nausea.

Murphry tried to see the man's hands, but he was wearing gloves. There were stains down the front of his shirt.

"To top it all off, I got laid-off yesterday afternoon. When I got home, all her stuff was gone from the apartment. I guess I'll be doing a lot of fishing for a while."

This is why I was instructed to camp here.

"That bitch has really got her hooks into you, Shawn."

The guy's name is Shawn.

"Look," the friend said, "when you're tired of feeling sorry for yourself and want to move on, let me know. Until then I don't have time for this crap."

As the friend gathered up his gear and walked off, Shawn just stared out at the river looking like he was about ready to jump in.

I have got to find a way to help this guy get free from that evil woman.

As the week progressed, D.D. Murphry, Secret Policeman, found it relatively easy to follow Shawn who was no longer a tall blonde fellow. He drove into the river front park a block away from the bridge every morning at five AM. He spent two hours fishing off the bridge, but never caught anything. Murphry was fairly certain there was no bait on his hooks. He just stared at the water, looking rather sad and angry.

When he started packing up his fishing gear, Murphry would grab a backpack of supplies and head for his little red motor scooter that he chained up every night behind a concrete barrier meant to deny access under the bridge.

As Shawn was pulling out of the parking lot, Murphry was following at a distance. He always drove to a little breakfast place and sat at a table outside and had a cup of juice and a donut, used the bathroom and left. *Very predictable,* Murphry thought. Then he'd drive to a parking lot across the street from a medical building and remain in his truck.

Murphry would sit under a tree nearby with a new romance novel he'd picked up at a local thrift store. He transcribed sentence fragments from the book into his notebook, then combined them and altered them until they made sense. After reading each message from his employer, he'd tear the sheet out of his notebook and eat it.

Shawn sat in his truck for hours at a time, occasionally using binoculars to look through the windows of the medical building. What he was looking for, Murphry could not say. He had consulted the romance novel on this matter and received the message, "A battle of wills takes place beneath. The ripples on the surface will not make immediate sense."

Murphry assumed this meant that Shawn and his girlfriend were fighting for control of his body and that Murphry would have to look past their immediate actions to their motivations.

Of course, she's skinny and he's really well built. Could be her motivation is that she wants a better body. But why is he coming to this medical building?

Maybe once she has taken complete control, she'll want to have a sex change operation to return her to her own gender. Perhaps she can get him to drive here and look through the windows, but she can't get him to enter the building and ask for the service yet.

Actually that's kind of far-fetched. Perhaps the truth is he wants medical help getting her out. He has control enough to drive here, but she won't let him get out of the truck and go in to ask for help.

The first day Shawn slapped the dash board a couple of times and let out a few expletives, but as the week progressed his anger escalated until he was spending several minutes at a stretch pounding the dash board and ranting at the windshield.

The battle is rising to the surface.

Late in the afternoon of each day, a voluptuous brunette woman in a white uniform, a doctor perhaps, walked out of the building.

She seems like a nice lady, (nothing like the woman in black), Murphry thought.

Shawn perked up each day when she appeared. He watched her carefully as she waited at the crosswalk for a break in the traffic, then crossed the street and entered the parking lot. She seemed to know he was watching and glanced frequently at his truck as she moved to a silver sports car, got in and drove off.

Immediately Shawn started his truck and followed. Murphry trailed him.

Shawn followed the voluptuous brunette wherever he could, to the mall, to the post office, to an apartment complex in the suburbs. When she went into an apartment there, he became very agitated.

Around 9:00 PM each night, he drove back to the garage where he parked his car and walked the two blocks to his apartment. Murphry worried about him until the next morning when he appeared on the bridge again.

On Thursday, Shawn's agitation escalated. At one point while sitting in the apartment complex parking lot, he pulled out a knife and gestured toward the windshield of his car and was saying something that Murphry couldn't make out. Then he put the knife to his own throat. Murphry wanted to intervene, but was afraid the man was in such an agitated state, there was no telling what he might do with the knife. Finally, he put the weapon away and broke down and cried.

The battle within him is almost more than he can bear. I think he wants to ask the nice doctor lady for help, but his girlfriend won't let him. I've got to do something and fast or this poor man is lost.

Murphry came up with a plan. Thursday morning, he loaded a syringe he found under the bridge with white gas from his Coleman camping stove. He followed Shawn to the little breakfast place. This time, instead of waiting at his scooter a block away, Murphry went in and ordered a coffee and sat near the fellow at one of the courtyard tables. When Shawn got up to go to the restroom, Murphry squirted the white gas into his glass of juice.

He came out of the bathroom and without sitting back down, Shawn dropped a couple of coins on the table, then lifted his juice glass and drained its contents. As soon as he pulled the glass away from his face, he looked like he was going to be sick. He spat out what little juice remained in his mouth and stumbled for the exit.

Murphry followed.

Shawn got within ten feet of his truck before he doubled over and vomited in the gutter. He retched until nothing but foamy stomach acid was came out, but there was no sign of his girlfriend.

Darn! Of course it wouldn't be that simple. He couldn't just puke her up. She must be spread throughout his system now. He remembered what Shawn's friend had said, "She's really got her hooks into you."

Murphry was so depressed he went to the library that afternoon to see his wife.

From a block away, he saw a woman in a black overcoat and sunglasses standing in front of the building.

It's her! She's definitely back, he thought, but still had some doubt.

From where he stood, he couldn't see her clearly enough to be absolutely sure, but he wasn't willing to get any closer for fear that she might see him. He hung out at a newsstand pretending to look at the magazines. Watching the woman, that unaccountable dread came over him once again. She was pacing slowly back and forth in front of the library, nothing more. So why did he find her presence so very menacing? It was confirmation. This *was* the woman in black or her replacement?

The woman looked at her wristwatch and took a look up and down the street. Murphry ducked behind the newsstand just before she glanced in his direction. When he looked again, he saw her walking away from the building, heading south.

Murphry assured himself that she was gone for good and then entered the library. He made his way to the Head Librarian, an older man named Mr. Oliver Ingram with a thin nose that always looked wet. "May I speak with Kate," he asked as politely as possible. Most of the staff here treated him very poorly because of the way Kate acted toward him.

"I'm sorry, sir," said Mr. Ingram, "but she is on vacation." He didn't even look up from his work.

Murphry decided not to ask where she had gone. He knew they would not know the truth. Obviously it is important to keep the truth from her husband as well. *She's probably on assignment somewhere.* He'd heard there was some trouble in the Middle East. *Perhaps she's there doing something exciting and useful.* This thought was all he had to allay his intense disappointment.

Murphry went to the restroom and when he came out, he saw Mr. Ingram talking with a woman in black. It was indeed Murphry's woman in black—the original one— he was certain of it now.

She must have nine lives, just like a cat! He remembered the photo from the French woman's trunk with the words "My Jaguar" written on the back.

Because she was leaning into the window of his office cubicle, she could not see Murphry. He ducked behind an acoustic panel and peeked around it to watch what she was doing.

To his horror, he saw her showing Ingram a copy of his high school senior photograph. Murphry was relieved when Ingram shook his head and said, "I don't recognize him."

Of course he would not, Murphry chided himself. *I am always in disguise.*

The woman in black thanked Ingram for his time and left the building.

Maybe I ought to follow her, Murphry thought, *and take care her once and for all. Surprise her and take her down.* But he was so shaken by her sudden reappearance, his legs were weak and his arms shaky. His chest hurt and his skin was clammy. He wouldn't be able to keep up with her, much less destroy her.

It is a good thing Kate was not here. This black cat woman might have identified her. She is getting too close to the both of us.

How he wished for his spoon. He imagined rubbing it with his thumb, again and again and again and again. Slowly, his heart eased and he felt control rise back up within his skin.

I have work to do. I must find help for the case I'm on. I was not called to be a Secret Policeman to waste time!

He sat at one of the computers and checked his e-mail. In one of the spams in his *In-Box* he found, *The boy was vacated dumpling sounds on and off willow switch old age home abbreviated insect despondent gristle bone twig.* This was not pertinent to the case he was currently on, but was part of the story of John and his grandmother's eyes. Murphry opened his word processing file concerning this case, made adjustments to the new phrases and pasted this into the crime story:

Now the boy was man and she had vacated the dumpling body and mind that could make him think sounds like an on and off willow switch. Living in an old age home, she was an abbreviated insect, a despondent gristle and bone twig wanting to die.

The story was still incomplete, but Murphry was encouraged. One day he would catch this John and restore the old woman's sight. But for now, back to the case at hand.

He read 64 pieces of junk mail without finding anything that might help. Finally, he read one from a law office offering assistance with divorce settlements. "Don't let her take half of everything," it screamed in large block letters. "We can show you how to hide assets. After all, possession is nine tenths of the law."

Murphry wondered about this expression. It was the only part of the e-mail that had any bearing on his case. It must be from his employer. He'd heard the expression, *possession is nine tenths of the law*, several times before.

Does it mean that if Shawn's girlfriend succeeds in taking over his body, there won't be anything that can be done legally to stop it? If so, then the clock is ticking.

Still, he needed an idea for getting the girlfriend out of Shawn. He used the search tool in his online browser to look for cures for possession. Most of what he found was religious crap. He didn't go in for that sort of thing. He did find stories in which those possessing were frightened away by a threat to the possessed person's life.

A fresh plan formed in his mind.

As he exited the library and turned toward the bus stop, three men dressed in police uniforms and the woman in black emerged from the shadows of the tree-lined south-facing wall of the structure.

He realized shamefully that he had not altered his disguise in over two hours.

The policemen spread out to encircle Murphry, while the woman in black stood to one side, obviously unwilling to get her hands dirty to help her subordinates. She opened her black attaché and extracted from it a vicious-looking weapon. It might have looked to others like an ordinary hair-care implement, but the dangerous curve of its handle and the bristling spikes that stabbed outward from it in all directions gave it away.

Murphry backed away toward the speeding rush-hour traffic. He was surrounded and she was coming for him.

But his employer was surely watching and would have his back. He'd just have to trust that they would bring all their power to bear on this situation as there was only one chance to get away and he was going to take it.

He turned toward the traffic and without looking, he dashed into it. A green Ford Explorer barely missed his backside as he rolled forward in a somersault between a silver Mercedes and a rusted out bondo-gray Nova. He came to his feet and leapt for the sidewalk on the opposite side of the street in one fluid motion. The belated honking of horns drowned out the protests of the policemen as Murphry ran down the street and into an alley that he knew would connect him with a street beside Taylor Park. He altered his disguise as he ran.

The True Government had pulled off the nearly impossible, he knew, and he was grateful.

Friday morning, Murphry got himself up and ready before Shawn pulled into the river front parking lot. By the time Shawn was in place at his fishing spot on top of the bridge, Murphry was on his scooter and ready to make his run. He waited for a pause in the traffic, then put the scooter into gear and started over the bridge, picking up speed as he neared the fisherman. He shouted, "It's out of control. I can't stop," but Shawn, a despondent look in his eyes, continued to stare at the water below. Murphry realized too late that the man was not going to look up in time to become frightened. By this time it was too late for Murphry to alter his course much without losing control entirely. He avoided hitting Shawn, but struck the bridge railing five feet away, took a header over the handlebars and found himself tumbling toward the river. Impact with the water knocked the breath out of him and he sank. He rose to the surface gasping and choking and clawed his way toward the river bank. When he got there, he found Shawn reaching to help pull him from the water.

When their hands clasped, something happened within Murphry that he'd not experienced for many years—he identified with another human being. Murphry imagined what it would be like to look out through Shawn's eyes, to have his feelings. In a flash, he got a taste of Shawn's likes and dislikes and had a sense of what it was to deal with the pleasures and pains of the man's life. He realized he liked Shawn and that he had not had such feeling for anyone but Kate for a long time. Now he was all the more desperate to help the man out of his terrible predicament.

"Are you all right?" the man asked, once Murphry was safely landed.

"Uh… yes," Murphry said, shaking off the reverie. "Are you?"

There was a light in the man's eyes Murphry had thought long gone. Does that light belong to Shawn or his girlfriend?

"Of course I'm okay. Let me help you back up to the roadway. I think your scooter is okay."

As they struggled back up the embankment, Murphry realized with some relief that Shawn hadn't recognized him from the breakfast shop yesterday. *I suppose he's been concentrating so hard on his internal struggle that he hasn't had much time to notice his surroundings.*

When they got to the top, Murphry found that his scooter was still running. One of the mirrors was missing, the paint was scratched in numerous places and the front fender was bent. Shawn helped him bend the fender back into position so it no longer rubbed against the tire.

Murphry wished Shawn could help him with his frustration. Without his spoon, he felt lost. He had not only failed again to help Shawn, but he had lost all dignity in doing so. He just hoped that no other Secret True Government employee had seen what happened.

Damn and double damn, D.D. Murphry, Secret Policeman, thought, but the voice in his head sounded like that of his aunt Martha.

Shawn had obviously had enough fishing and took off after helping Murphry.

He finally caught something. I guess he's quitting while he's ahead.

Murphry followed him. Instead of going to the breakfast place, Shawn stopped at a hardware store and bought a pistol, then drove to the medical building parking lot.

As Murphry sat under the tree with his romance novel, he thought about what Shawn's purchase of a pistol meant.

He's about ready to give up, but his girlfriend might be able to stop him. If he succeeds in turning the gun on himself, should I try to stop Shawn, or let him end his misery?

As the morning passed and afternoon wore on, Murphry had difficulty answering this question. He watched Shawn intently, hoping he would not have to make the decision.

Once the girlfriend had complete control, there wouldn't be much he could do about it. As far as he knew, possession of someone's body wasn't a crime. If the expression, possession is nine tenths of the law, meant anything, it could be that simply by the possession alone she'd be afforded certain rights and protection under the law. In that case only a secret policeman could make things right.

Surely there was some other way to get this evil woman to vacate Shawn's body. He racked his brain looking for the answer.

In the late afternoon, the brunette doctor appeared across the street. As she waited for a pause in the traffic, Shawn got out of his truck and approached the cross walk. But was it Shawn propelling his body? Murphry could see the bulge of the pistol in his pants pocket.

The girlfriend is going to murder the doctor to prevent Shawn from seeking her help.

Murphry got to his feet and hurried toward Shawn, not knowing what to do.

The Doctor noticed Shawn and her back stiffened. She turned her eyes away. *Does she sense she's in danger?*

I must prevent this murder, even if it means harming Shawn.

The girlfriend reached into Shawn's pocket and began to draw the gun out. The doctor caught the movement and went into a crouch.

Murphry was ten feet away.

"Shawn," Murphry called out, but the man ignored him.

She has complete control.

Murphry was almost on top of Shawn as his girlfriend raised the pistol and the doctor turned to run.

Why didn't I see this coming? I'm too late.

Out of the corner of his eye, he saw the express bus approaching from the left at a high rate of speed.

He heard a gun shot when he slammed into Shawn. It was all Murphry could do to arrest his own forward momentum and avoid being hit. Shawn's body flew into the path of the onrushing bus and passed beneath its wheels.

The bus obstructed his view for only a moment, its tires screaming as the vehicle was brought to a halt.

Then Murphy could see the doctor again. She lay in a spreading pool of blood.

Tears streaming down his face, D.D. Murphry, Secret Policeman, ran for his scooter, started it and fled the scene. There would be no honorable trophy from this case to send to Kate.

The next morning Murphry's memory had been revised:

Out of the corner of his eye, he saw the express bus approaching from the left at a high rate of speed.

He collided with Shawn before his girlfriend could pull the trigger. It was all Murphry could do to arrest his own forward momentum and avoid being hit as Shawn's body fell into the path of the onrushing bus and passed beneath its wheels. He heard the doctor cry out in horror, then the scream of tires as the vehicle was brought to a halt. The bus obstructed Murphry's view for only a moment. Then he could see the doctor, running back toward the medical building.

She was unhurt.

Murphry didn't want to see what lay in the street. He turned away and ran.

Tears streaming down his face, D.D. Murphry, Secret Policeman, made it to his scooter, started it and fled the scene.

He was thankful for the revision, whatever its source. He knew this was all Kate would ever hear of it and that made him feel a little bit better.

Fragment: Friends Like These

3:55 PM—Monday, December 19th

D.D. MURPHRY, SECRET POLICEMAN, was headed for the bus stop at 23rd and Gilcrest, about to start his daily "Bus Duty," as he liked to call it. He would ride several buses aimlessly, watching the general public, exercising his authority secretly where need be.

He missed Kate. Either she was still on vacation or he just hadn't figured out her new schedule yet. He'd stopped asking the staff at the library about her because he was certain they would not give him the truth or didn't know it themselves.

The loneliness I'm feeling, he told himself, *is for sissies.* He shook himself to try to get it out of his system.

Squinting against the cold winter wind, his eyes lit upon a message in the text of a newspaper lying on top of a stack at a periodicals vendor. It said, "She will see you if you don't watch your step." The sentence was pieced together in his mind in a flash from subtly bolded words scattered throughout a block of text.

Noticing a streetlight glowing up ahead, he realized that the text was referring to the woman in black. He crossed the street to avoid being seen. Most would not even observe that the lamp was lit in broad daylight. Even he might not have detected it if he hadn't just been warned. Those who did notice it would probably think the mechanism that automatically turned the light off when there was daylight was broken. Murphry knew better—the streetlight was a surveillance device used by the False Government. The woman in black would be using it at that very moment to try to locate him. As long as he didn't walk on the section of sidewalk it shone upon, she would not see him.

At the bus stop, Murphry stood alone with his thoughts and feelings. He shook himself again, trying to dislodge the lonesome feeling.

A Secret Policeman doesn't need any friends. The work is too dangerous—your friends might get hurt—and it would be easier for the False Government to get to you through your friends. The False Government depends on the capricious loyalty of family and friends. I can only hope they never find out about Kate and me.

A taxi passed him with a toe-nail fungus medicine advertisement on it. It said, "With Friends like these, who needs enemies?"

And that was the real problem with friends and family—you'd end up trusting them and inevitably they took the opportunity that that presented to stab you in the back. Human beings just weren't to be trusted.

The fact that Kate was also a Secret True Government employee and couldn't be seen with Murphry without risking her cover being blown was probably the only thing that had saved their marriage. He knew that the divorce rate was well on its way to becoming one hundred percent. What did that say about spending time with your significant other? No, as difficult as it was to accept at times, his employers were wise to have mated the two of them and then found cause to keep them apart.

The bus arrived and Murphry boarded. Once again, he was able to sit in the rear of the bus so he could study the other passengers. They were an unassuming bunch, he thought until he turned and looked more closely at the man beside him. The fellow had excessive nose hair. It was a dead giveaway of the hypochondriac. His ilk cost the American public millions of dollars every year and put a strain on the health care system.

"What can you do about it?" Murphry gathered this message from the mass transit regulations posted near the front of the bus, the ad on back of a magazine, and a candy wrapper lying in the aisle. The message seemed to be a test of sorts. His superiors kept him on his toes by asking such questions from time to time.

Nothing, because it is daylight. If it were night time, I'd come up behind the guy, grab him by the neck and haul him into a dark alley where I could dispatch him. Then there'd be one less hypochondriac putting stress on the system.

"Your nose," Murphry said to the man.

"Pardon me?" he said.

"Your nose," Murphry said again. "Is it real?"

"Of course it's real." The fellow gave him a quizzical look and turned away.

"There's dandruff on your shoulder," Murphry said.

The man pretended to ignore him.

"Your clothes are wrinkled and your hair is greasy."

Several of the other passengers, hearing this exchange, became curious. Murphry knew he was getting through to them. No doubt some were the fellow's friends and family who were unaware the man was such a danger to society. Murphry meant to change that here and now. It wouldn't take much.

After taking stock of the other passengers who were all staring, the man turned to Murphry and looked him in the eye. "I have been ill," he said slowly and carefully, obviously trying hard to control his emotions. "I have not been able to keep myself up as well as I might."

"Aha!" Murphry nearly shouted.

The man jumped in his seat. Several of the other passengers started as well.

The bus was about to stop at Hyacinth Avenue, Murphry's stop. He got up, looked around at his audience and said, "You all heard him. You know what he is now and you know what to do."

As he stepped off the bus through the side exit door and back into the winter wind, he imagined them all jumping the hypochondriac and tearing him limb from limb. That wasn't likely to happen, unfortunately. The type of justice Murphry had just set into motion moved much slower. But now that these people had been apprised, their disapproval would set in. They'd talk amongst themselves and it would deepen. The man would be ostracized, especially by his friends and family. His life would become a living hell and eventually he might save everyone a lot of trouble by taking his own life. One way or the other, he'd be so marginalized that he would no longer matter.

This would take a while, but Murphry could be patient. He had taught himself how.

Friends and family are good for something after all, he told himself.

Picking Her Brain: Case #6

11:02 AM—Monday, January 2nd

D.D. MURPHRY, SECRET POLICEMAN, sat in his cubicle at the library, gathering notes from his e-mails. Over the last few days he'd found four phrases that were clearly a part of the unsolved case of John and his grandmother's eyes. Murphry rubbed his hands in satisfaction, looked over his shoulder to see if Kate might be watching (she wasn't), then reread the revised clues that were pasted into his case file.

His love for his grandmother was a lumpy bindle-stiff that refused to chant. A misty death rumor, his growing hatred visited her every part. All but the baubles in her head. His clubfooted johnny cakes still rose and fell whenever he saw them.

Next, Murphry added the phrase he'd just discovered today, *beat whimsy sticks but no good*. He altered the phrase and pasted it into the file:

He would beat her with whimsy sticks, but it would do no good.

Better, but still incomplete, he thought, frustrated. In his pocket was the key to his scooter, which was parked outside beneath the library front steps where no one could see it. He rubbed the scooter key, though it did not offer the same comfort as his spoon had. It was cool to the touch, and then warm with the rubbing, just like the spoon. It was smooth on the side, and his finger glided easily over it, just like the spoon. The key to the scooter had served him well, just like the spoon had served him well. But his thumb was not happy with the change, and refused to give him the warm relief the spoon had given, the same slowing of the heart and easing of the blood.

Another test, he thought, from the True Government. Metal, he supposed, was just metal. When you stripped it down and rounded it into an eating utensil or cut it into a motor-starting implement, it was still, at its heart, metal.

But then again, maybe it wasn't. Maybe the word "key" and the word "spoon" by their very natures changed the actual makeup of the metal. Maybe skin on his thumb and skin on his forefinger, though both skin, were actually very different things by virtue of the additional moniker "thumb" and "forefinger." He would think about that when he had more time.

He sighed and let go of the key.

His beloved, Kate, appeared to be missing. Over the days that the False Government promoted as "holidays"—Christmas, Chanukah, Kwanzaa, New Years— he had assumed she was on an extended mission for the True Government. She was bright and she was beautiful. Why shouldn't they put her to work in some clandestine mission? She certainly wouldn't be on vacation again so soon. No, she had been sent off to do something important, surely.

The library had been closed for the last few days, and was reopened now for the first time in the new year. A new year was rife with new possibilities in crime solving, but Murphry didn't feel the enthusiasm as strongly somehow.

He couldn't stand not having Kate around. He missed having her furrow her brows and bare her teeth in his direction. He missed the dismissive turn on her heel and the hitch of her lip when he came into the library.

How long does the True Government plan to have her out on assignment? Will they ever let her come back? Has she told them that she has had enough of me? Is she now acting as a librarian at some other city's library, in some other state? Russia or Spain or Portugal or Egypt, perhaps? Maybe she is no longer a librarian, but is now a blonde cashier at a grocery store or coffee shop in Paris. Then what will I do? How can I find her? No, no, they would have to bring her back here. My devotion as a Secret Policeman has earned me at least that!

It all weighed heavily on his mind and in his gut.

He forced his thoughts back to the e-mails. He found himself reading the parts of the spam that made sense. Sometimes messages were hidden here as well.

"Koko Petroleum is our next hot pick! Koko has an opportunity to become involved with veteran oil people in the development of this field that has been combining technology with vast resources most successfully."

"Dear Friend, I am contacting you privately with a matter of most possible urgent and serious importance of about money that I have had since the killing death of my father, Premiere Jhadi Memah, special assistant to the vice president of Nigeria. It is with grateful appreciation and thanks to the grace of God that I have discovered you and that I now ask you to help me transfer a sum of $4,000,000 into an American bank account such as the one that you currently have at your place of which you live and bank. Please respond to me in confidential message so we can begin the process. Be careful that no one knows of this as it is secret between me and you."

"Before we start with the profile of NNFC we would like to mention something very important: There is a Big PR Campaign started today. We are already seeing movement it will go all week so it would be best to get in NOW."

"When was the last time you had an erection you were proud of, one your girlfriend would look at and say, 'Oh, honey, is that there big beeee-ooo-tee-ful whopper for me?'"

"So you've been bankrupt? Don't be left out of the fun! You, too, can have a new unsecured credit card with the help of our friendly agents at Ajax Finance. A new set of furniture? No problem! A shiny set of wheels? Why not? A vacation to Hawaii? Just let THEM try to keep one out of your hands! Don't let financial frustrations and roadblocks keep you from what you truly want out of this life! This is where we step in!"

Murphry automatically chose the right words and phrases to jot down and rearrange. When he was done scrawling he had come up with:

"Dear Friend, there is an opportunity to have help from our agents. A matter of urgent importance, this is where we step in. There is a big campaign NOW. Just let THEM transfer a shiny set of wheels for your girlfriend. That there beeee-ooo-tee-ful whopper has become involved with veteran oil people. Be careful; possible killing, death, roadblocks. You can have a new life, combining technology and resources. Why not? Try."

Murphry sat back in his chair and rubbed his eyes. This message was very violent, whatever it meant. *Death* and *killings*!

The teenaged girl in the cubicle next to him cut a long, sputtering fart, glanced over at Murphry, and giggled.

"Oh, man, that stinks!" she grinned. "Sorry 'bout that!" She was a tall and lanky girl, with spiky auburn hair, a row of studded earrings parading up her lobe and a gold loop dangling beneath her nose. She wore a short skirt and a well-oiled leather jacket that creaked when she shifted positions.

"It's supposed to stink," said Murphry. "It is a waste product. A gaseous waste product, actually." Didn't they teach high schoolers anything anymore? And speaking of which, why wasn't this kid in school? It was the middle of the day.

The girl rolled her eyes and turned her attention back to the computer.

"Why aren't you in school?" Murphry asked. He didn't mean to be rude, but maybe this was another holiday he didn't know about. He needed to be kept informed about such things.

But the girl ignored him, and picked up where she had left off with the mouse and keyboard. Murphry couldn't see around the cubicle wall to see what the girl was doing on the computer, but he guessed it was some sort of game with the intensity of the clicking and tapping.

Maybe the girl doesn't go to school. Maybe she was kicked out for doing something terrible. Or maybe she is a lazy girl and just quit. Maybe the other kids make fun of her because of her strange jewelry. She smells like French fries. I bet she has a job in the afternoons, working at one of the local fast food restaurants, serving all that artery-clogging crap to unsuspecting people! Perhaps that is my next case. Stopping this girl from killing people with burgers and fries and oily apple pies!

"Marla?"

It was Oliver Ingram whom Murphry didn't really care for. He was standing behind Marla, tapping her on the shoulder. Marla looked around and didn't seem angry that she had been disturbed.

"Any luck there?" Oliver asked.

Marla said, "No, Uncle Oliver. I don't think I'm going to find what I need on the computer."

Uncle? So this grouchy old man has family?

Murphry leaned way back in his chair, pretending to stretch, and glanced over at Marla's computer screen. There wasn't a game there, but a map of the city. It looked like an old map, from a hundred years back, perhaps. She also had a notebook open, with lots of scribblings on the page.

Marla closed her notebook and stuck it in her backpack. Murphry eased his chair back down and stared at his own screen.

"I might have found something that will help you," Oliver said. "If we still haven't got what you need in the local history room, the next step will be to pick Kate's brain for the information."

Murphry's heart, vessels, hair, and skin all froze at once. It felt as if he had been suddenly freeze-dried like coffee on that old television commercial. *Kate! The old man Oliver knows where she is! She isn't on a secret mission! Oliver has kidnapped her and is holding her in a secret place! Is he—is Marla—False Government or is this casual criminality?* There was no way to determine this at the moment.

"We'll get it, don't you worry," said Oliver. "I'm very impressed with your dedication to this project. I bet you'll get first place."

"Maybe," said Marla, shouldering her pack. "I'm not worried about the prize so much. I just want to get it right. Finding out and mapping where the city officials of the 1920s stored their booze is pretty cool."

"Spoken like a true historian," said Oliver.

The girl shrugged and smiled slightly. "Maybe," she said. Then she and Oliver moved down between the tall shelves of books, heading to the other side of the library.

Murphry leapt to his feet, knocking the chair back onto the floor. He scooped it up and back into place, and then hurried along the aisle parallel to Oliver and Marla. He dogged their steps, following along by the hushed sound of their voices.

"Kate will know," said Oliver. "She's one of the smartest ladies to ever be on our staff. If it's anywhere, it's in that brain of hers."

"Cool," said Marla.

The old man, Oliver Ingram, and Marla are going to get into Kate's brain with a pick! They are going to dissect her like a common frog for information they can't find anywhere else!

Murphry reached the end of the aisle, and then peered carefully around the tall shelf just in time to see the librarian and Marla turn in the other direction and stop in front of a door marked *Local History*. The old man pulled a set of keys from his pocket, selected a particularly nondescript one, and jammed it into the lock. With a determined wiggle, he unlatched the door and it swung open. The two of them entered. The man shut the door behind them. Murphry went to the door and pressed his ear to the wood. He could hear nothing.

The room is soundproof! Naturally it would be soundproof! They need a place where they can talk in private!

Where is my beloved Kate? Is she locked up in the old man's house? Of course, that is where she is! She is in his basement, or his attic if he has an attic, or in a closet or pantry if he has neither basement nor attic. She is there at his mercy, right where he could pick apart the beee-ooo-tee-ful gray and white matter inside her precious skull to find out... to find out what? To find out... the truth!

Murphry reached into his pocket and began to thumb the scooter key frantically. The ragged edge dug into the skin. *But no,* he told himself, *Kate is much too smart, too savvy, to let them get into her thoughts. She maintains good thought discipline. She knows how to lock her mind away just like Oliver Ingram has locked her away. They will learn nothing from her. But I have to save her. I have to set her free, without anyone knowing it was me who performed the rescue. I can't let on no matter what! I have to leave here as calmly as I came.*

But Kate will know and she will love me for it!

He would spy on the library, and watch for the old man leaving. Then he would follow him home and rescue dear Kate.

Adjusting the muscles of his face so they revealed no emotion, Murphry went to the library's front door, took a moment to paw casually through the giveaway bin of paperbacks as a ruse, and then strolled outside and down the steps. He even smiled to confuse those who were coming up the steps. *Good move. They suspect nothing.* Fishing the scooter key out of his pocket, his trembling hand let it go, and it dropped off the steps. The key struck a small rock, *pinged* in the sunlight, and vanished in the dead grass. Murphry hurried down to retrieve the key and his scooter.

But the scooter was not under the steps anymore.

Someone has stolen my wheels!

Murphry stood out on the sidewalk, looking up and down the street, watching and listening for a flash of red or the hum of the engine above the other sounds cutting through the cold winter morning. No, it was gone. Long gone. Some lazy, fat person stole it, had hot-wired it and rode off just as proud as a pea. Or some kleptomaniac who couldn't keep his paws, and his buttocks, off of other people's things had tossed it in the back of a pickup truck. Murphry hoped the thief of the scooter had family who did not approve.

He stooped down to look for the key. He did not see it. Running his fingers carefully through the tall, yellowed blades, he came up with nothing.

Darn! Both the key and the scooter?

Murphry ran back up the steps and looked down where he thought he'd dropped the key. He squinted, watching for a glint of metal. There! A flash near the purple winter pansies someone had planted in mulch near the library's sign.

Back down on the ground, Murphry clawed the key from beside the pansies. He held it tenderly, then stuck it in his pocket and let his thumb work back and forth on the side. Tension began to melt along his arms and legs. He was in control. He was capable. He would figure out the message and free Kate before they picked her brain.

Suddenly, the key didn't feel like a key anymore. The ridges had vanished and had been replaced with a smooth, concave cup. Murphry tugged the key from his pocket. It was no longer the key. It was his spoon.

How did I get my spoon back? What happened to the key?

But it didn't matter, really. It was just one of those things. He had to rescue Kate.

There was a bus stop shelter with a bench across the street from the library. Murphry would sit on it and watch the building. It was dreadfully cold outside, and the heavy pewter clouds overhead threatened snow or sleet, but Murphry had other business to attend to. The weather was not his concern. Luckily there was no wind, just the bone-chilling air.

As he waited, he read his message slowly, over and over. Maybe there was more to it, clues he had not received yet. A bus pulled up to the stop, several old ladies climbed on, and then it drove off. The advertisement on the bus's side promoted an upcoming Spring Jazz Festival at the Park. "Many famous featured musicians! Arnie Reginald! Brian Danson! The Alley Boys! New Orleans-style cuisine! If you don't come, you'll be missing the year's biggest music event in the city!" The only word that leapt from the bus into his head was "missing." He jotted it down. A wet, detached magazine cover was slapped up against a nearby light pole. Murphry leaned over to see what it said. It was a copy of Mac World, a catalog rather than a magazine. Black and red letters described the goodies to be had inside. "The Newest Macs, a Complete Guide! The Best iPod Add-Ons!"

"Complete" was the word that he selected to add to his message. Now it read:

"Dear Friend, there is an opportunity to have help from our agents. A matter of urgent importance, this is where we step in. There is a big campaign NOW. Just let THEM transfer a shiny set of wheels for your missing girlfriend. That there beeee-ooo-tee-ful whopper has become involved with veteran oil people. Be careful; possible killing, death, roadblocks. You can have a complete new life, combining technology and resources. Why not? Try."

Clearly, Marla, the teenager, was the veteran oil person. She worked at a fast food restaurant, dipping potatoes in oil and serving them up to people who had little care for their health. Kate was the beeee-ooo-tee-ful whopper, with her lushly padded hips and abdomen, and now, without her consent, she was unwillingly involved with Marla. The True Government was telling him that there was an opportunity to have help from them, even though there would be the danger of killing, death, financial frustrations, and roadblocks.

But what does the rest mean? The shiny new set of wheels for my missing girlfriend? Who is THEM? False Government agents? Someone else? Am I losing my ability to interpret words? No, that's impossible! His heart thudded in his chest. His head hurt.

He watched the library from the bench for the rest of the afternoon, hoping it would come clear, knowing it would soon if he was patient. But patience, when it came to thinking about Kate's safety, was hard to hang on to.

Marla and her Uncle Oliver came out at the same time, as the clock on the bank down the block read 3:52. Murphry tucked his notes into his jacket and watched the two out of the corner of his eye. As they stood on the corner waiting for a break in the traffic, Marla zipped up her leather jacket and Oliver buttoned his heavy wool overcoat. Both wore expressions on their faces that told Murphry they had not found the information they wanted for their secret "project." They would have to pick Kate's brain now. It was inevitable.

The woman in black rounded the corner of the library building. Murphry froze. He watched as the woman approached the two and began talking to them. Murphry pulled his head back into the bus stop enclosure and watched through the scratched plastic wall as the woman in black seemed to show Oliver and his niece something on a piece of paper—perhaps the picture of Murphry she'd shown Ingram once before!— they shrugged and nodded their heads. The woman walked away.

She's probably telling them to keep their eyes open for me. Ingram didn't recognize me from the high school photo before. Hopefully Marla won't either.

Murphry hoped they would cross the street to ride the bus. Then he could ride with them. He would disguise himself with another clothing adjustment. But no, they crossed the street and climbed into a shiny, silver PT Cruiser, complete with a sunroof. Was this to be Kate's new car, perhaps? No, it was much too flashy for her. The license plate spelled "BOOX4U."

What the heck was that? It's not a word at all. How pathetic that a librarian can't even come up with something for his license plate that makes any sense. Might as well just let the DMV come up with their own gobblety gook.

The Cruiser pulled away from the curb and headed north. Murphry stood, staring after them, his face cold, his heart seething.

It constantly amazed him that people would be willing to have their phone numbers and addresses in a big book for anyone and his mother to see. Yet, here it was, a whopping collection of white pages with thousands of names and numbers. There had been no phone book in the phone booth at the nearest corner—someone had taken it off its chain long ago—but there was one at the gas station/convenience store near Franklin Park. The girl behind the counter had shoved the book in his direction, as if she was afraid her fingers might touch his and contaminate her. That was good. He preferred not to touch or be touched. Touches, he knew well, could bring on strange feelings that a Secret Policeman should not have to tackle.

Seven Imlers. Two Indarts. A quarter page of Ingersolls. Four Ingertos. Three Ingraham. A half page of Ingrams.

There. Oliver Ingram. In cold ink. His home address. 1524 Catton Lane.

Murphry wasn't sure where Catton Lane was, but it would be an easy find. A bus pulled up to the stop by the park. Murphry pulled his jacket collar up to disguise himself, and he climbed on. "How long does this bus take to get to Catton Lane?" he asked the driver.

The driver shook his head and said, "Don't go to Catton. You need to take the bus from the Broad Street stop next to that art center, that'll get you to Catton."

Murphry nodded. As he turned to get off the bus, he saw two young people near the front, dressed in their brown and yellow fast food uniforms. Both girls, one thin like Marla and one huge like a toad. Murderers! But he hadn't the time to deal with them just now.

It was a half-mile walk to Broad Street, through the park, past a spate of hotels and office buildings. The sky was nearly black when he reached the bus stop, and his hands were blue by the time he climbed aboard a bus and dropped his coins into the slot to pay his fare. He slipped to the back and then studied the map on the wall over the seats. Catton Lane. There! A short street, only four blocks long, in the city's northwest. Murphry stared at the map, careful to prevent anyone from knowing he was staring. Which block was home to that devious librarian and his murdering niece? Which block held his beloved wife? From the map, he surmised it would take approximately twenty-seven minutes to reach Catton, if the bus driver was obedient to his route as shown by a red dotted line. Each block was about a minute, adding on an additional thirty seconds for each stop along the way.

The bus jerked, whined, and began to move. Murphry sat and clutched the window frame with the fingers of his right hand. He rubbed the spoon with the thumb of his left hand. In the glass of the window, he saw his reflection sharpening, dimming, sharpening, dimming, as the riders near him played with their reading lights.

Kate, I'm going to save you.

Kate, hold on, my dearest. Don't let their probing reveal anything!

Outside, the world was navy and slate, punctuated with garish oranges and yellows in the guise of advertising signs, "Open All Night!" "Allie's Coffee, Best Served Hot!" "Morton's Funeral Services!" "Wayland Multi-Plex Theaters!" None of the signs gave him more information. He had to go on what he'd already gathered.

Warm air piped back across his face, and the man next to him began to snore softly. Murphry let his eyes flutter closed. He forced them open but they closed again, and then he saw her on his inner lids. Kate. His Kate. His beeee-ooo-tee-ful smiling Kate.

They were on a beach, together. It was dawn, and the sun swam the horizon in a pool of fluorescent hues. Little white crabs scuttled on the sand, weaving words in the damp. "Patience." "Motivation." "Reward."

Kate, her hair free and blowing in the wind, her clothing now a sheer, light fabric that hugged her delicious curves, turned to him and held his face in her hands. "Thank you, my dearest, for everything. Everything. Everything." She kissed him on the lips, and the sensation was both thrilling and agonizing; he felt as if he was flying into the sky, he felt as if he were crashing down like that falling fool of a skier on the opening sequence of the Wide World of Sports, a television show from his childhood.

She moved her face from his, squeezed his hand gently, and led him toward the water. He noticed he was barefoot, and his toes obliterated the words the crabs continued to scratch out in the sand. They reached the shoreline, and, holding hands, stood as a wave in the distance crashed, leveled, softened, and then reached their feet. The salty liquid was warm, like bath water. Passion rose in him, and he turned to his wife, gathered her in his strong arms, drew her to him, crushing her perfect breasts against his chest…

"What the hell are you doing, asshole?"

Murphry's eyes sprung open. The complainer was the man beside him. Murphry had wrapped his arm around the man's shoulder and had drawn him close.

"Nothing," said Murphry. He withdrew his arm, shoved his hand into his pocket, and began grinding flesh against metal…*back and forth and back and forth and back and forth.*

"You just keep your perverted hands to yourself or I'll call the cops!" The man snatched up his briefcase and clambered up the aisle to a seat near the middle. On the way, he tripped over the extended leg of a nursing mother, who squawked in pain and drew the baby away from her chest. "Watch it, man!" she complained. "You're not the only one on this bus, ya know?"

"Do that Earth-Mother-stick-out-your-boobs-and-feed-your-brat routine in private, why don't you?" yelled the man.

Murphry thought the man was an idiot for making such a big scene. Now everyone was looking at him, instead of Murphry. *Good.*

The bus pulled over to the side of the street. Murphry squinted out the window to see which stop it was. But there were no benches, no bus stop sign. Was the bus driver going to toss out the man who'd tripped on the nursing mother's leg?

The intercom system sputtered. The riders sat straight, at attention, waiting. Then the driver spoke. "Ladies and gentlemen, I'm sorry to report that we're having engine trouble. I'm going to have to radio in to the main office for another bus to come replace this one. It shouldn't take long, no more than half an hour or so. I apologize for this inconvenience."

This is the roadblock! I can't wait an additional half hour. What if that half hour is the difference between Kate's brain remaining intact and it being picked to shreds? I have to walk. I have to run! Why did someone have to steal my scooter?

He got off the bus with five other angry riders. It had begun to drizzle, a cold, bone-carving sleet that drummed his head and shoulders. Three of the riders stormed off in various directions. The other two, elderly women in conservative coats, little wool hats, and lapel pins—one a dragonfly, the other a jeweled flower of some sort—remained.

"I'm going to just catch a cab," said one elderly woman to the other. "I have to get home quickly. I'm baby sitting this week for my grandchildren. They got off from school more than two hours ago. I don't like them being home alone for long. Do you want to chip in, Darlene?"

Darlene said, "You bet, Annie. I don't care to hang around on a bus for what the driver promises will be a half hour, but, knowing how well things go in my life, it will be at least an hour, or longer."

Murphry recalled a portion of his message. *There is an opportunity to have help from our agents. A matter of urgent importance, this is where we step in.*

Could these women be the ones assigned to step in on his behalf?

"Where are you ladies going?" Murphry asked the women.

"Spring Street," said Darlene, but then her friend poked her in the arm and then put her gloved hand to her mouth. *Of course, Darlene wouldn't want to say that too loudly; others nearby might hear her. And there are a couple guys over there, standing outside the restaurant having a smoke.*

"Spring Street is adjacent to Catton," said Murphry, lowering his voice to protect his words from prying ears. "I can share that cab, too."

"Well…" said Darlene.

"Sir, I'm afraid there won't be room enough for three," said Annie.

Good, they are playing the game cautiously. "I can sit in the front with the driver," said Murphry.

"Well…" said Darlene.

Annie patted her lips again, her eyebrows drawing up into a look of feigned concern. Then she stepped cautiously into the street behind the bus and waved down a taxi with a flap of her delicate little old hand. She and Darlene quickly slipped into the cab, and as Murphry reached for the front passenger door he saw Annie tapping the driver vigorously in the shoulder. *She's going to ask him if it's okay if someone sits up front*, thought Murphry. *I know it is. I've seen it done. He'll never have an inkling as to what is really going on.*

Murphry opened the front door and climbed in. He nodded at the women in the back, who offered him what would appear to the driver in the rearview as pained smiles. Then he said, "Let's go."

After giving the driver their destinations, they rode in silence, save for the garbled messages that came through the drivers' speaker and the short, one-word answers given back. Silence was best. Silence was golden, so said Simon and Garfunkle in a song whose tune he had long ago forgotten. In a short eight minutes—Murphry began counting the seconds once the driver had put foot to pedal—the cab pulled up to the corner of Spring and Catton. The driver hawked a lougie into a wad of handkerchief and said in a raspy voice, "That'll be 9.85."

"That's… just over three dollars and twenty-eight cents each," said Annie. She and Darlene dug into their purses while Murphry shoved open the door and hopped out. The old woman needed to check her figures again. It was just over four dollars and ninety-two cents each. Agents sent to help would certainly cover the bill of their assistance.

"Sir, oh, sir…?" called one of the old women from the cab, but Murphry kept on walking. There was no need to go back to hear their words of support and encouragement. They knew he needed to get to Oliver Ingram's house with dispatch.

Many of the homes on Catton were still living in the past, still celebrating Christmas, with twinkling holiday lights bordering doors and windows, giant Santas and reindeer anchored along driveways, and heavily trimmed trees visible from uncurtained living room windows.

Murphry found Oliver Ingram's house in short order, a story and a half "split level" that had been all the rage of builders back in the 1960s. There was a wreath on the door and white candles in each front window. The Cruiser was nowhere to be seen; in the garage, most likely. There was little vegetation around the Ingram home. Just a couple spruce trees and one large, naked oak or maple or some sort of deciduous. No place to hide and observe. He would have to just go on in without taking time to surveil.

The chain link fence that separated the backyard from the front was an easy scale, but the door leading into the garage from the back was locked. One thing he'd never learned to do was to pick a lock. He'd never had to. His assignments had never required such a skill.

I wonder which is harder, picking a lock or picking a brain?

This thought made his stomach turn over on itself, and he quietly spit bile onto the ground.

There was a window in the door. This was his best bet. He listened carefully for several minutes, determining from the muffled laughter that someone in the house was watching television. He was surprised a librarian would allow a television in his house. Murphry knew well that television not only took people away from reading books, but it was one of the worst abusers of words there had ever been. A medium that should have respected words for their power, it used them for its own purpose. Sports, sitcoms, dramas, news, documentaries! Murphry wasn't sure how he knew this...at some point in his life he had vague memories of watching television but the memories were distant and cloudy...but he did. He also knew that one day, words would turn on television and there would be hell to pay.

I'm glad to be on the right side of words.

A dog next door spotted Murphry, and pressed its nose through the split rail fence and began to bark. What dog-words were those? What was the dog trying to say? Was he warning Murphry of impending danger? Was he trying to alert Ingram to the man who planned on breaking into his house? *Will I ever understand all the words out there? All the languages? If I do, then I will be the greatest Secret Policeman that ever lived.*

Assuming the dog was part of the False Government, Murphry tiptoed to the fence, scratched the dog behind the ears a few times, and then bashed it on the head with a rock. The dog fell onto its side and remained silent.

Back at the door, he waited until he heard a particularly loud burst of laughter from the television set inside, and then cracked the window with his jacket around his fist. He wasn't worried about a security alarm. Ingram wasn't rich enough for that. Then Murphry reached through the broken shards still in the wood, unlocked the door, and made his way into the garage.

"Kate?" he whispered as he stood next to the silent PT Cruiser. "Kate, are you in here, my dearest?"

There was no reply. Ingram and his hideous niece would surely have her bound and gagged so she could not cry out. Murphy moved cautiously about the oil-and-cleaner-scented garage, looking behind and inside every box that was large enough to hide a human. Kate was not there. The Cruiser had no trunk, so it was easy to see she was not in the car.

She's up in the house itself. That is where they can keep closer tabs on her.

The door to the interior stairs was not locked, but it squeaked. Murphry froze, tilting his head, listening up the steps. No one came running. No one turned the television down. He waited another minute, counting down the seconds. Then he went upstairs.

The steps led to the kitchen, an ordinary little room with yellow floor tiling, a white valance over the window, and a little round table in the center. The refrigerator was mottled with countless magnets—plastic fruits, credit card sized advertisements, a little Santa head and Easter Bunny, tiny owls with google eyes, flowers. In the sink was a pile of dirty dishes, likely from a recent supper. A microwave clung to the wall over the stove. A battery-powered can opener lay on the counter next to an empty can of cling peaches. Stealthily, Murphry checked the refrigerator and the cabinets. No Kate.

Where are you, my love?

He opened several drawers slowly, and it was then he realized this was no ordinary kitchen but a chamber of horrors. In one he found barbecue tools, including a long-handled, two-tined fork and shish kabob skewers bundled with a rubber band. In another was a package of "fondue forks;" smaller than the barbecue fork but just as vicious and deadly. In another drawer, amid commonplace flat wear, he found pickle forks and a box half filled with toothpicks.

They are prepared for their heinous deed, no matter what size picks it will require! But I will never allow it!

Under the sink was a box of mouse poison. He pocketed the box. It could come in handy.

Off the kitchen was a half bathroom with the door standing open—Kate was not in there, Murphry could see without even leaving the kitchen. Beyond the bathroom, down a short hallway, was the living room. There was a commercial running at the moment, one for a local fast food chain. "Say double bacon ranch combo with cheese, please! And make it a biggie!"

"Marla, mute that please." It was a woman's voice from the living room. An older woman's voice. *Marla's aunt, Oliver's wife*, Murphry determined. "All that noise makes my head hurt!"

"Sure," said Marla. And the television went dumb.

So there were three of them, then. Three he would have to outsmart.

"How is the history project coming, honey?" said the aunt.

"Ah, man, it's harder than I thought it would be," said Marla. "I still have a week to get it done, but I'm not finding everything I need. I spent hours in the library today but could only find a few maps from the time period I want. The microfilm had some helpful leads but then I hit a dead end. I suspect the guys had vaults under their houses but I need letters or diaries."

Murphry could hear the old woman shift in her seat. He saw a flicker of shadow on the living room floor as she did so. Then the woman said, "I think it's wonderful that the area home schoolers are going to be allowed to take part in the city's history and social science fair next month, along with the public school students."

"Yeah, I guess so."

"I'm proud of you, honey. I know your mom and dad would be proud, too."

"Yeah, I guess so."

So where was Oliver? Could he already be in one of the upstairs rooms, picking Kate's brain with a fondue fork? There was no way Murphry could get around the rest of the house to search for Kate without going through the living room and being seen. *What do I do now? Kate!*

And then the phone rang.

The phone was in the kitchen, mounted on the wall next to the basement steps.

"I'll get it," Marla said.

Murphry rushed to the stairs and made it down three before Marla entered the kitchen. He could not go out because the door at the bottom squeaked and she would hear it for certain. So he pressed himself up against the wall, as flush as his body would go. The pounding of his heart was so loud, he was afraid it would rattle the walls. But it didn't, or if it did, Marla didn't hear.

"Hello?" Marla walked to the refrigerator with the phone. Murphry could see her from the shadows. She opened the door and took out a soda, popped the tab, and took a sip. "Yeah, Kate, it's good to hear you. Uncle Oliver said you'd been sick for almost a week. That sucks, big time. You feeling better?"

Kate?

After a pause, Marla said, "That's good. You keep drinking water and eating chicken noodle soup. That's what Aunt Pam always tells me." Pause. "In two days?

That's good. Everybody at the library misses you. Hey, when you do get back, would you have some time to talk to me about my history project? I need a couple new leads. Uncle Oliver said we should 'pick your brain.' Doesn't that sound nasty? I say we just talk." Marla chuckled, then paused. "Yeah, I'm chasing down the old boozin' councilmen!"

Was Kate at her own home, then? Was she really sick, and not here at the Ingram house? Was she truly safe, and only wanted as a resource?

It could be a trick! Marla can be pretending it's Kate on the phone in case the kitchen is bugged!

Marla wandered over to the open doorway to the garage steps. She was a mere three feet from him now. Murphry flattened himself even more, though the box of mouse poison made an uncomfortable lump. Marla turned her back on the doorway and leaned against the jamb. She said, "Don't worry, I'll make sure Uncle Oliver wears his glasses next time he re-shelves."

There was a laugh on the other end of the line, close enough for Murphry to hear it. It was Kate's laugh. He knew her laugh. He hadn't heard it often, only two or three times as she never laughed when she saw he was around, but the sound of her laughter in his head was like a key in a lock. Only she sounded like that. No one could reproduce such a beautiful sound.

Marla is talking to Kate! Kate is at her home! She is all right!

"Yeah, okay, Kate," said Marla. "I'll talk to you later. Get some rest!"

Marla left the doorway and Murphry could hear her hang up the phone. Then she left the kitchen.

Kate is safe!

Murphry's tightened heart eased a bit. He felt himself smile. But then the smile locked on his face.

But is she really safe? Maybe it wasn't really Kate. Maybe it was a recording of Kate's laugh!

Murphry went back into the kitchen. He moved to the phone, removed it from the wall, and pressed the call-back button. It rang twice and then Kate answered. "Hello? Hello?"

Kate! It is you!

"Marla, is that you? Marla?"

Murphry hung up the phone. Kate was all right. He was disappointed that she had been unable to witness him performing the rescue. Somehow he had missed it as well. Murphry didn't know for certain how he had thwarted the deadly plan, but he had. Ingram and his niece were not involved with the woman in black and perhaps had no connection to the false government at all.

Ah, he thought. *Ah.*

He snatched up the battery-run can opener beside the empty can of peaches and dropped it in his pocket next to the mouse poison. He'd never had a battery run can opener before, always the hand crank. This was the new technology for his life. He smiled, and could see himself smile in his reflection on the glass of the microwave.

Then he took the steps to the garage and sneaked back out through the door. Behind him, he heard the phone ring. Kate was calling back to see who had tried to reach her. It didn't matter. She was safe.

The next-door neighbor's dog was stumbling about groggily in its yard. Murphry leapt over the fence and walked out to the street. The air smelled fresh and the cloudy night sky had opened to let bright stars peek through. Part way down the block, however, Murphry hesitated. A nagging phrase rose up in his mind, one he'd not dealt with in his message. *The shiny new wheels for my missing girlfriend. How will she get shiny new wheels?* But suddenly he laughed and shook his head, because he'd forgotten the important word in the phrase. *THEM.* Let *them* do it. "Them" would be the True Government, of course. *Them* would reward Kate soon with shiny new wheels. They just wanted him to know it was going to happen, so if he saw her leaving the library in a new car that he didn't recognize, he wouldn't worry.

He patted the mouse poison in his pocket. He had a new assignment to take care of. The cab had passed a fast food joint a quarter mile back. Not a long walk at all. It was time to do something about those murdering short order cooks who served up heart attacks in buns and in little cardboard French fry containers. A bit of this in the saltshakers would hasten the inevitable and bring a little attention to their oily, fatty crimes. To make an omelet you have to break a few eggs.

It was a good saying.

Fragment: A Gag Gift

3:43 PM—Thursday, January 5th

NOW THAT HE WAS certain Kate was safe, it was time for Murphry to deal with his nemesis, the woman in black, once and for all. She had a hand in so much of the False Government's nasty business, Murphry was beginning to think that perhaps she was in charge of the organization or at the least controlled that within the city itself—all the more reason he should waste no time in getting rid of her.

From the cover of the bus stop shelter across the street, he staked out the front of the library. He'd sat here all day yesterday without seeing the evil one, but because this was where he had seen her the most he kept his vigil. He was certain she would show up soon. She was a woman with a job to do and would retrace her steps until it was done.

While he waited, he took notes from his new paperback, a book titled, *Your Dreams and What They Mean*. Murphry didn't remember his dreams very often. When he did, they were about things like doing laundry or riding the bus—not much to interpret, at least nothing that would help him be a better Secret Policeman.

Of course the subject of the book didn't matter. What he was looking for were directions on how to dispose of the woman in black. None of the words in the book popped out at him, however; not one called to him more than the others. So, anxiously and hopefully, he picked random fragments from the first sentence of each page and jammed them together into sentences.

On his pad of paper he wrote, "I wore a new pair of pants around my waist and down each leg with a rough stone," and "She wove pigs and cows into chickens while wrestling an alligator into boat," and, "Having not bathed, his body was a scattering of warm, stinky manholes," and, "The gag gift left me vomiting on the floor."

This was good. Now he had choices. He could wear her down, transform her into something else, clean himself until he was untraceable, or trick her with a gag gift.

That was it! In order to get her in a vulnerable position, he would trick her.

A gag gift, hmm...? A gift that makes you gag. He could use such a thing to get her attention from a distance.

Murphry saw some dog feces lying on the sidewalk nearby. He dug a brown paper bag out of his jacket pocket, squatted next to the dog waste and used a stick to flip the turds into his bag. With a crusty blue marker he'd tucked in his shirt pocket he printed on the bag, "For the Woman in Black." Then he ran across the street and placed the bag on the third step leading up to the entrance to the library and returned to his spot on the bench in the bus stop shelter.

Most people entering or leaving the library just gave the sack a wide berth as they negotiated the stairs. A couple of street people inspected the contents, but Murphry scared them away by shouting at them, "LEAVE THE SACK ALONE!"

Eventually Murphry nodded off out of sheer boredom and fell off the bench. This awoke him and he got up, dusted himself off and looked across the street at the library. His employer had awakened him at just the right moment—the woman in black was approaching his gag gift. She seemed to be considering what was written on it and then she risked a peek at its contents.

Murphry didn't know how this was going to get her attention, but he had followed the instruction he'd received from the True Government and he knew he must trust them to know what they were doing.

Sure enough, she seemed to gag and then withdraw from the bag. She straightened and look around, her hand to her forehead.

This was his chance.

Murphry stood and stepped out of the bus stop shelter, raised his hand and waved at the woman in black.

She caught sight of him, paused... then began to make her way across the street in his direction, glancing back and forth for traffic.

Murphry received such a jolt of adrenalin he felt as if he'd swallowed his heart. He turned and walked away. Now he must lead her to a spot where she'd be vulnerable. He had just the place in mind and although there was no way he'd forget where it was, his thoughts were so frayed on the edges that he wasn't sure he could get there.

It's only eight blocks away. Focus, Murphry told himself. He just had to make sure that he kept the right distance from the woman in black. He didn't want her too close until they got where they were going. Before he made any turns, he glanced back to make sure she could see which way he was going. Each time he did, she looked a bit closer. He'd speed up, his heart leaping up into his throat. He'd swallow it back down.

Just before he reached the Haven Street Bridge, he ducked down and bolted ahead so that she'd lose sight of him. He got to the barrier put in place by the bridge authorities to prevent people and bums from going under the bridge and crouched down behind it, watching her. She walked out onto the bridge looking right and left and right and left for him.

Murphry took off his belt and looped it in his hands. A nice leather garrote. That would complete the gag gift. He passed under the bridge and emerged on the other side, climbed the slope, crossed the street and sneaked up behind her.

But then his foot struck a pebble. It pinged into the bridge railing. The woman in black spun around as he was about to bring the belt into position and she raised her weapon. The tiny spikes that bristled from it were so tangled with hair that it looked as if she'd used it to brain her last victim.

"You—" was all she had time to say. Murphry knew in an instant that his belt was useless while she faced him. He stiff-armed her in the shoulders and she tumbled over the railing with a startled squawk. She struck the water with a great splash and sank. The current quickly carried all evidence of her impact away under the bridge and out of his sight.

Murphry rushed to the other side of the bridge to see if the woman in black could be seen going down river. She wasn't there. He looked as far over the edge as he could to see under the bridge, but couldn't see her there either.

The river is so cold, there's no way she'd last for long.

"I saw you do that." The voice came from the other end of the bridge. It was Ned Guthrie, a homeless man Murphry knew from Under Blunt. They had never gotten along because Ned filled in crossword puzzles with whatever words he could get to fit whether they belonged or not.

"I'm going to call the police," Ned said matter-of-factly. "You're a murderer!"

What did he see down there? Does he have knowledge that the woman in black is indeed dead? It is not the sort of thing someone would lie about.

Before Ned drew more attention to what happened, Murphry needed to make his escape.

His heart swelled with a sense of accomplishment as he ran.

Change Your Mind: Case #7

9:30 AM—Wednesday, January 11th

D.D. MURPHRY, SECRET POLICEMAN, trusted his employer would apprise Kate of his dramatic dispatch of his nemesis, the woman in black. A great weight had been lifted from his mind with the demise the evil one, and of course, the return of his wife to the library. He looked forward to life again. He enjoyed all the routines that he had worked so hard to install in his life; visits to the library to check his e-mail, daily bus rides to monitor the activities of the general public, collecting cans for the True Government and going to the post office to pick up his checks.

However, his visits to the Post Office weren't as pleasant as they used to be. Nearly every time he went lately, he saw fat Harold Posen standing outside the building asking people to sign various petitions. Murphry didn't like him. He was part of the obesity problem, for one thing, and his skin had a grayish cast to it which made Murphry think of old meat that had been left out in the sun too long.

But what Murphry hated most about seeing the fat man was that he was always raising issues Murphry didn't want to think about, such as whether or not same-sex couples should be allowed to have the same rights that other couples had, whether or not the False Government should be able to sell your home and property if you're not making them enough money, and whether or not public school teachers should have religious influence in the lives of the children they taught. The man could go on and on about such things because he was very obviously bored and lonely. It all went in one ear and out the other for Murphry. *Same sex couples must mean the partners both have male and female sexual organs, or maybe it means they both enjoy the same type of sex. Who cares about such things?* Murphry decided he would feel sorry for Posen if he were capable of it.

Even today, in the cold winter drizzle, the fat man was outside the Post Office. "Sign my petition against citywide video surveillance," he said, holding up a clipboard full of signatures. "They want to put cameras at every intersection."

Murphry knew who *they* were—the False Government—and he would have like to have signed this petition, but couldn't because leaving a paper trail might lead to his undoing. He said, "No, thank you."

"Okay, true, I'm paid for each signature I get for that one," Posen said, "but here's one I really believe in." He lifted another clipboard and offered Murphry a pen. "Forget that other petition about not having cameras. This one says we *do* want video surveillance at every intersection in the city. This will help the police catch all the filth that walks our streets."

Filth, huh? Now Murphry had to stop and think about that. Living primarily on the streets, he rarely got to take a full bath or shower, but being a representative of the True Government, he felt he had an obligation to keep himself well-dressed and groomed. He regularly went to the charity stores to pick out fresh clothes. Sure, most of it was ten to twenty years old, but he liked to think he looked quite dapper. He most often bathed at a water fountain or restroom sink, using a rag or sponge. He never showered at the shelter. A Secret Policeman could not chance what might happen, what secrets might be revealed, while so vulnerable. When he felt he really needed it, he'd strip off all his clothes in the dead of night, when no one was awake to see him, and bathe in the river under the Haven Street Bridge. Cleanliness was the least of his worries.

Murphry was shaking his head, about to walk off, but the fat man continued. "They'll be able to visually identify wanted criminals."

Murphry paused again, but quickly decided that his outward appearance was not an issue either. He was in the practice of avoiding video surveillance and knew there were times when it was unavoidable. His way of dealing with this was to look unassuming and average. There was a time when he had been much taller and thin as a rail. Through concentration and good diet, he had reduced his height and gained some weight. The problems of being caught on film were solved by his subtle disguise shifts throughout the day; turning his collar up, rolling his sleeves or pant legs, shaving the hair off his arms and legs or walking with a pronounced limp—the possibilities were endless.

Murphry turned away.

Posen raised his voice a little higher. "They'll be able to sniff them out and track them to their hide-outs more easily."

Now here was something to worry about—a camera with a sense of smell. Although Murphry kept himself very clean, he was certain that he always smelled of iron. He liked to think he smelled this way because he was a strong and capable agent of the True Government, but he suspected it was because he had blood on his hands.

He didn't like to think of the innocent people he had harmed while fighting crime. The euphemism for it was "collateral damage," but he knew they were human beings with lives and loves. There was a time when these thoughts did not occur to him, and even now, he did his best to push them from his consciousness whenever they occurred. His fear was that his feelings for these innocents might cloud his thoughts and distract him at the wrong moment. If this were to happen during a hot pursuit, a criminal might get away.

Murphry was most successful at banishing these thoughts just after catching criminals and making them pay for their crimes. But, inevitably, and more and more frequently, these thoughts and concerns returned to him.

He blamed people like Harold Posen for making him think about things he didn't want to think about. *Damned sympathy monger!* Why should he care what the average man or woman on the street thought or desired? Who were they in the scheme of things? The True Government knew what was best and he was their instrument. He would do his job and try to keep his mind shut.

But if Harold Posen got his way and the False Government was able to catch his crime fighting efforts on film, then everyone would see them on the evening news. The newscasters would talk about how Murphry smelled and everyone would know who he was and what he was up to. His cover would be blown. If he lost his position as a Secret Policeman, he wasn't sure he'd want to go on living.

Harold Posen was indeed an evil man, a tool, a secret employee of the False Government. Perhaps he had been hired by the False Government to destroy Murphry because the woman in black had failed. If so, killing her had done Murphry no good at all.

Whatever the case, Posen would have to be destroyed. But Murphry didn't want to kill this man. When he'd knocked the woman in black into the river he'd been threatened by a drunk bum who claimed to have seen what happened. That wouldn't be the case again. There would be nothing to witness and no threats to make. Instead of ending the gray-skinned man's life, Murphry would demoralize Posen and undo his credibility in the eyes of the False Government. *Perhaps they will be convinced that hunting me costs them too much and will decide to cut their losses.*

There was only one thing Murphry could think to do at the moment to hamper Posen's effort. He reached for the clipboard Posen was offering.

"I knew I could change your mind," the fat man said.

He was sure Posen expected him to accept this as a manner of speech. But coupled with the dark smile on the man's face, Murphry knew that the fat man would remove and replace his brain given the chance.

As Murphry tucked the clipboard under his arm and took off running, Posen shouted stupidly, "Hey, you son-of-a-bitch, that's mine." Murphry could tell the man was chasing him although he didn't turn to verify it. As fat as Posen was, it wasn't difficult to outrun him.

Now he had to figure out how to discredit and demoralize Harold Posen. The first thing that came to mind was to drive him crazy, literally, by making his life hell.

Surreptitiously Murphry watched Harold Posen for the next two months, learning everything he could about the man. Since Posen had no car, it was easy to follow him. He walked or rode a bicycle and never traveled far from home. He lived alone in a converted car garage in the side yard of a large stone house on Apple Tree Drive near the Post Office. If the name on the mailbox was correct, the elderly couple living in the house went by the name of Kaufman, but Murphry rarely saw any evidence of them. Holed up, he thought, as he saw over time that all the necessities for their continued existence were delivered.

The property was hemmed in by hedges growing out of control. This provided Murphry with plenty of cover for his surveillance. Just outside Posen's door was a fenced in area of the yard where two very friendly Beagle dogs stayed when they were not indoors with the fat man. Their names were Mister Belvedere and Lurch. It was easy for Murphry to make friends with them. Ever after they did not bark when he approached, but demanded much petting. He bought them bird feeder suet, made of beef tallow and seed, and fed it to them each day until they would eat no more.

They gained weight rapidly, would not eat the food Posen fed them in the evenings and farted constantly. They were no longer welcome indoors. *Now he'll be even more lonely and pitiful*, Murphry thought.

What Murphry could discern of the man's activities inside the house was limited by the wedges of view he had through the two windows, one in the front of the garage which faced east, the other set in the south-facing wall of the structure. The place was really one big room divided unevenly by lightweight partitions into roughly four different rooms: a living room, kitchen, bedroom and bathroom.

The fat man seemed to have no friends, no one important in his life. For entertainment he listened to the radio or read. He apparently did not own a television, which impressed Murphry. He wrote inspirational messages—no doubt propaganda from his False Government employer—on a little chalkboard hanging in the makeshift kitchen area. During moments of stress, he would stand before the board and read the message aloud.

Murphry stole Posen's mail every day. Going through it, he learned that the man received monthly disability checks—secretive payments from the False Government— that he worked for various activist groups who paid him to round up signatures for petitions, that he was chronically late paying his bills and that he had a grown daughter, named Naomi. Murphry read only enough of Naomi's letters to determine who was writing and what her relationship was to Posen. He returned the junk mail to Posen's mailbox, but kept the disability checks, the checks from the activist groups, the bills and the letters from the daughter.

Murphry took a part off Posen's bicycle every day, starting with the smallest and most insignificant and with time moving on to more important ones.

Discovering that the garage had its own water main shutoff in the front lawn, he made a habit of shutting it off each day. It took Posen a while to figure out that the shut off in the yard was where he had to go to turn the water back on.

While the man was out each day, Murphry would go to work on his home. He climbed on top of the garage roof and used a screwdriver to poke holes in the roofing so it would leak when it rained.

After a heavy downpour that must have soaked the fat man's living space, Posen had a long talk with his landlords, the Kaufmans, and soon someone came by to fix the roof. The next day Murphry went back up on the roof to undo the repairs. For good measure, he broke two of the garage windows by throwing stones through them. It took a week and another talk with the Kaufmans before Posen got glass and glazing compound and fixed the windows. In the mean time, Murphry filed down one of the window locks so he could pop it open with his screwdriver from the outside. Now he'd be able to work on the inside of the house while Posen was away.

Murphry deduced from looking at Posen's bills that the garage apartment had its own connection to the power grid. He became impatient waiting for the electric company to shut off the man's power and broke in through the rigged window and turned on all the lights, opened the refrigerator door and turned his electric heater thermostat up as high as it would go. He cut holes in the pockets of Posen's pants.

The inside of the garage apartment was a pigsty, trash everywhere, dishes piled in the sink, dirty clothes all over the floor, the smell of sweat and garbage almost overpowering. *Obviously the False Government will employ any sort willing to do their bidding.* It was a real eye opener for Murphry, but he quickly reigned in his contempt. *I should be careful not to underestimate those who would destroy me and all I stand for.*

Restless while waiting for Posen to return home that afternoon, Murphry scanned the letters from Naomi, the daughter. Once again, he tried not to concentrate on the words too carefully lest they open up a world of meaning in which he might become lost. One paragraph caught his attention because it seemed to confirm what Murphry knew about Posen's personality and gave some indication that he'd communicated to at least one person the effect Murphry was having on him.

Naomi had written, "Why would anybody have it in for you? You've always thought your ideas and opinions are so important people should listen to what you have to say. You force your ideas on people too polite to tell you they don't want to hear it. That's why you have no friends. It's why I live on the other side of the continent and only communicate through the mail so you can't argue with me. What you're telling me about all the mishaps in your life sounds like pure paranoia. You're just not so important that anyone would spend this much time screwing with you."

She doesn't know about his involvement with the False Government.

Beyond the most immediate information the letter provided about Posen, Murphry began to identify with the man's loneliness. Recently the Secret Policeman's visits to the library to see his wife had only deepened his emotional isolation. Kate was ignoring him completely now. If he spoke to her, she refused to respond. No doubt she had been instructed to do so, but it was becoming increasingly difficult for Murphry to ignore his feelings. Identifying with Posen only made it worse. This sympathy is exactly the sort of thing that had caused Murphry to decide to undo the man in the first place. He cursed himself for reading the letter.

When Posen returned home that evening, he opened all the doors and windows to air out the garage. Ranting about the heat, the smell, the violation of his privacy, he carried his garbage out to the trash cans beside the Kaufman's house. Murphy watched him look over his home, inside and out. He did not discover the rigged window.

Posen called to his dogs, but they would not come to him. He found them lounging by the side of the house and he fussed at them for being fat slobs incapable of frightening intruders away. Mister Belvedere had had the squirts all day. Posen slipped in a patch of it and went down. He got up cursing, wiped the greasy fecal material from his clothes and retreated into the garage.

Murphry felt sorry for the dogs. *I must start feeding them properly.*

Disgusted with the free ride the electric company was giving Posen, Murphry broke into the garage the next day and turned all his breaker switches off and left the refrigerator door wide open again. Today he did not turn the water main off. He flushed Posen's dirty underwear down the toilet until the drain stopped up. He stoppered the shower and kitchen sink and left the water running in both when he left the garage.

That evening after a row with his sink, toilet and shower, Posen had a loud argument with the Kaufmans on their front stoop. The only part Murphry heard clearly was Posen saying, "Rent control is the law. You can't get around it by trying to drive me out. It won't work."

They retreated into their home and the fat man returned to his living quarters. He must have called for help because two policemen arrived and looked over his home briefly. Murphry was ready to take off through the bushes should they begin to inspect the yard, but they did not.

Speaking to the officers, Posen gestured toward the Kaufman's house. He stamped his feet, waved his arms and shouted.

Murphry feared for the old man and woman, assuming the policemen would react vengefully against them on behalf of their fellow false government colleague. Instead, the officers seemed to be trying to calm Posen down.

Posen yelled at them, "Aren't you going to check out the property for evidence of an intruder? Won't you assholes at least check for finger prints?"

One of the officers got right up in the fat man's face and seemed to be warning him of something without raising his voice. Then they both left.

Murphry also followed Posen to and from the Post Office and watched him periodically as he went about the collection of signatures. As Murphry's sabotage of the fat man's life escalated, he could see the effects on Posen's health and demeanor. He was nervous and his skin was grayer than ever. He perspired heavily even in the cold weather and there was noticeable weight-loss. His face became pinched, his expressions hardened as he squinted with evident suspicion at everyone, including the people he approached for signatures. This made folks nervous and so he got fewer and fewer signatures as time went on.

Murphry learned to duplicate the man's handwriting so he could alter the inspirational messages on the chalkboard in the kitchen. He changed "Am I not destroying my enemies when I make friends with them," a quote he recognized from Abraham Lincoln, to read, "Am I not destroying people when I make friends with them." He felt remorse at having altered this great man's words, but knew it was for a good cause.

One afternoon, Murphry was about to alter another message on the chalk board when he heard a key slide into the front door lock. He had just enough time to slip into a curtained closet. Posen was back from the Post Office early.

Murphry watched through a tear in the fabric of the curtain as Posen entered, dripping blood from several patches of road rash on his left knee and forearm. His bicycle had finally come apart on him, Murphry decided. Posen was mumbling, "I understand now," and "It's all good." Color had returned to his skin. Perhaps it was just the effects of the injury.

Posen stood in front of the chalkboard, took a moment to composed himself and then read aloud, "The task ahead of us is never greater than the power behind us." As Murphry recalled, there was no attribution attached to this quote.

The fat man walked to his easy chair and sat down, turned on the radio and tried to find his favorite stations, but Murphry had just today reassigned all the radio buttons.

Posen went gray again. He leapt from his chair and shouted at the house, "Whoever you are, come on out. Show yourself." He dashed out into the yard, still calling for the intruder to reveal himself, his voice rising higher and higher, becoming louder and louder. Mister Belvedere and Lurch began to bark. Posen was in the yard for some time tearing through the bushes, looking for the intruder.

Murphry took the opportunity to return to the chalkboard and alter the inspirational message.

"I won't be mad," Posen was shouting. "I understand now. Just show yourself. We can be friends." Murphry approached the window through which he could see that Mr. Kaufman was standing by his front door, watching the fat man raging in his side yard. He turned and seemed to be saying something to someone, Mrs. Kaufman presumably, inside the house.

After a time, Murphry saw a police car pull up in front of the house. He was in a panic to get out, but he was trapped. He kept his position by the window as long as he could, but as the officers were getting out of their car and Posen was headed back into the garage, he dashed for his hiding place behind the curtain.

Once again the fat man stood in front of the chalkboard, composed himself and read the inspirational message aloud, "The task ahead of us is never as great as Posen's powerful, large behind." His shoulders sagged and a tear slid down his cheek. Then the color returned to him again and a smile spread across his lips.

"That's funny," he said.

Posen turned around and went out to meet the policeman. After some conversation with the Kaufman's, the officers put Posen in the back of their car and drove away.

D.D. Murphry, Secret Policeman, had completed his task—the False Government had arrested its own secret employee. He was certain they would deem him so emotionally unstable that they would release the fat man from their service.

Within days, a junk truck came by Posen's place to clean his stuff out of the garage and a sign was posted on the structure that read, "For Rent." Murphry never saw Mister Belvedere and Lurch again.

One month later Murphry sat down for an evening meal at the Fifth Avenue soup kitchen. He was surprised to discover Harold Posen seated in a wheel chair, directly across from him. He hadn't recognized him because of the man's dramatic weight-loss.

Looking at how gray Posen was, Murphry had a sudden, undeniable twinge of guilt for what he had put him through. It prompted him to speak to Posen. "Good evening, Harold," he said.

"Do I know you?" Posen said, looking up.

Murphry averted his eyes. "You used to do petitions outside my Post Office."

"Oh yeah, I remember you. You never signed a damned one."

When Murphry glanced across at him again, he saw that Posen was looking at him with his eyes squinted up hard and brow wrinkled.

"Something wrong?" Murphry asked nervously. He wanted to get up and find another seat, but they seemed to all be taken.

Posen's hard appraisal broke and he sagged a bit. "Lost my best friend is all."

Murphry decided he meant he'd lost his job working for the False Government.

"Damnedest thing," Posen went on. "When I was going through it all, it was hell—the hardest two months of my life."

Murphry knew now he must be referring to his sabotage.

"Thing is, it was the only time in my life when I felt the least bit important to anyone. Someone was paying very close attention to me, and then suddenly—whoever it was—my friend was gone."

Murphry was doing his best to concentrate on his soup, but then he felt the man's eyes on him again and he slowly lifted his gaze to see Posen staring hard at him.

"You're that fellow who stole my clipboard, aren't you?"

Murphry didn't answer, returned his eyes to his soup.

"It all started after that…" There was a far away sound in Posen's voice as if he were reviewing memories.

Murphry risked another look. Posen was sitting up straight now, the color had returned to his skin and he was smiling.

Startled by this, Murphry stood up from the table.

"You're the one, aren't you?" Posen asked, leaning across the table and extending his open hands toward the Secret Policeman.

Murphry backed up until he bumped into the woman seated behind him. "Watch out," she bellowed.

His eyes were fixed on the ardent expression on Posen's face. As far as he could remember, no one had ever looked upon him with such tenderness. How he longed for Kate to look upon him with such an expression.

"What is your name?" Posen said, trying to maneuver his wheel chair around to the other side of the table.

For a split second Murphry wanted to allow himself to receive that affection, to explore it, hold it close and claim himself worthy to receive it. He might pretend it was a gift from his wife.

Murphry almost said his name.

The next instant he knew it was all a trick, a lie.

A trap set by the False Government—they only pretended to arrest the sympathy monger and now he's redoubled his efforts to destroy me.

Murphry backed his way into the aisle between the tables and headed for the door.

"We could be friends," Posen called after him. "Really, I'm not angry with you."

As D.D. Murphry, Secret Policeman headed for the exit, he struggled to take his jacket off and turn it inside out. By the time he hit the street, he had put it back on again and was certain no one would recognize him. He wormed his way into the night.

His Grandmothers Eyes: Case #1, Part 2

4.30 PM—Wednesday, April 22nd

At last! I've found the final few clues to the mystery of John and his grandmother's eyes.

Murphry nodded with great satisfaction. Now that the story was complete, it read like this:

"The one-eyed devil only sees in one direction," his grandma would say and point out the two eggs embedded in her face. Like her words, they were round sparkling ones that bounced around in their sockets. They were god-peeping and blood-busting alive. He thought the best most people could do was paw at the dirt just inches from her face.

Along with the glossy orbs, Grandma sported six blue and purple sawmill tattoos, and her skink experiments had once saved the toenail industry. Back in the day, a mere glimpse of the bony plates of her wedding gown had caused 1920s megaphone crooners to swallow their own heads. Even when he was raised, she could still fire lap dogs from her armchair at blinding speeds. Spite for this was a waterproof woman who could not actually swim.

Now the boy was man and she had vacated the dumpling body and mind that could make him think sounds like an on and off willow switch. Living in an old age home, she was an abbreviated insect, a despondent gristle and bone twig wanting to die.

His love for his grandmother was a lumpy bindle-stiff that refused to chant. A misty death rumor, his growing hatred visited her every part. All but the baubles in her head. His clubfooted johnny cakes still rose and fell whenever he saw them. He would beat her with whimsy sticks, but it would do no good.

One night he made it past the muggy, wet nurse who was his grandmother's shadow. Grandma was stretching and yawning the dog saw and did not awaken even as he scratched away the socked grubs of her head.

He made out with his prise.

To cover his tracks, he Fed them to himself, then went to pick them up.

A mistake, this led him to his pissed office box where he met his match and maker.

Now he had to recognize the story in the world around him. This would lead him to the perpetrator, John. Then, of course, it would be a simple matter to locate and relieve the suffering of the victim, John's grandmother.

Murphry left the Library and went to check his mail, walking the ten blocks in order to give himself plenty of time to think.

It was dark by the time he got to the post office. The clerks were gone for the day and the lights turned down low inside. Good thing they allowed access to the boxes after hours, but Murphry thought the place potentially dangerous once the sun had set, the complex halls lined with post office boxes being something like a labyrinth of dark alleys where one might easily be waylaid. When here at night, he always checked behind him and listened for others who might be just around the corner. Murphry saw only one other person inside this evening, a woman of about forty, slightly overweight.

He had a sudden thought, a realization, really, that he'd be combating global obesity soon. Fat people caused a lot of problems.

Murphry's box number, 42205, was, as far as he knew, a meaningless string of digits. Then, with sudden insight, he realized that his box number was today's date and he smiled. Still, he had to make two right turns and one left in the labyrinth to get to it. What was the purpose in that?

He opened his post office box and pulled out his paycheck.

As he was opening the envelope, the fat slob of a woman was leaving. He could hear her as she stopped and addressed someone near the entrance.

"John, good to see you. I didn't know you used this post office. How have you guys been?"

"Deirdre, nice to see you," came a man's voice. "We've been fine."

Murphry needed to get a look at this John right away. *Patience*, he told himself.

"We've recently moved into the neighborhood," the man said. "Grandma Evelyn needs assistance these days so we wanted to be close. Her eyes, you know."

"Well, its good to see you. Have Karen call me, would you?"

"Sure."

Murphry pretended to consider his check as he heard the door shut and the man's footsteps approaching. He glanced up in time to meet John's gaze.

They exchanged good evenings as the fellow walked past. There was just enough light for Murphry to see that the man's eyes were green with flecks of brownish red in them. He recalled that the evil crone had referred to the color as "paprika."

"A mistake, this led him to his pissed office box where he met his match and maker." He remembered this line from his efforts at the library today.

Everything has come together. Everything has put me in the right place at the right time to solve this crime. Now this *will impress my beloved Kate.*

After suffering her forced coldness for so long…Murphry could almost feel her nakedness pressed against his own.

John was headed to a box even farther back than Murphry's. Murphry watched him turn the next corner. There was a convenient slice of shadow just this side of that corner. John would have to return the way he had come.

Now D.D. Murphry, Secret Policeman, understood why his P.O. box was set so far back in the labyrinth and why he had a spoon in his pocket.

Interlude: The Handwriting on the Wall

2:46 PM—Thursday, April 23rd

D.D. Murphry, Secret Policeman, was on his way to mail the trophies to his wife when the woman in black caught up with him again near the Post Office. Now he was running, pounding down one stretch of sidewalk after another, but knew he could not elude her for much longer. Although she was almost three times his height and twice as broad, she demonstrated unnatural speed and agility as she chased him through the streets. *She is a cat, a black leopard,* he thought as he exited an alley and ran along Dumont Street, glancing back. And of course, like a big cat, she had her claws retracted as she ran. But he knew she had stashed that bristling weapon, that deadly tool she had tried to use on him twice already, in the black attaché she clutched to her chest. There was no telling what other lethal force she kept hidden beneath that dark, flowing overcoat. No doubt she was heavily muscled like those shiny women he'd seen on body-building shows. She probably even knew martial arts.

But she is dead and gone! his mind cried, as if by the intensity of the thought he might make it true again.

Murphry rounded the corner onto Ketter Avenue and the package containing the trophies flew out of his jacket pocket and seemed to vaporize in mid-air. He knew that this could not truly be what happened, but he could not see where the package had gone and had no time to look for it.

He cast about quickly, looking for escape. On his side of the street was the second hand store, and the door was propped open with a chair. A "Welcome—Everything 20% Off" sign hung at an angle on the door glass. He dashed inside and made his way toward the back of the store through rows of tables and boxes full of junk. He bumped into the proprietor as he passed through a doorway into a back office. The proprietor grunted and snarled. Murphry bounced against the door, ripping the sleeve of his new lime green leisure suit on a metal sign that read "EMPLOYEES ONLY."

"Hey, you can't go in there," the man said, recovering his balance and reaching for Murphry.

Spinning around to ward off the store owner, Murphry glanced through the office door, over the man's shoulder and up the center aisle. The shadow cast by the woman in black had reached the front of the store and was pouring through the front doorway. Murphry twisted out of the proprietor's grasp. And then the woman caught up with her shadow and put her hand to her eyes to stare into the store. Before she could see him, Murphry dashed through the office and exited through a door at the back of the building. He found himself in the alley again. Murphry slammed the door behind him and backed up against it in case the woman in black or the proprietor were to try to open it.

Running wasn't helping. She was obviously more powerful than he was and she would eventually run him down. His disguises didn't work on her anymore. Murphry needed somewhere to hide. He knew he should move to the right this time. He pulled up his right sleeve and consulted the freckle map on his forearm. At first, with his heavy breathing and the trembling of his body, he had a hard time locating himself on the map. He'd just had a bath this morning in the bus station restroom and some of the lines he used to connect the dots were a bit faint. Then he recognized his position—indicated by a pulsing blood vessel beneath a pale spot of skin—and the lines began to make sense.

There—a phone booth, represented by a rather rectangular freckle. It was two blocks away. He'd head for that.

Murphry ran down the alley. Just before making the right turn onto Centre Street, he glanced back the way he had come. As far as he could tell, the back door to the second hand store had not opened.

Good, Good!

Murphry dashed along Centre Street, turned left, ran down the next length of sidewalk and turned right at the intersection. There was the phone booth. *Good good good!*, he thought. It was the old fashioned kind with four walls and a ceiling. But wait. It was on the wrong side of the street. Had it been moved? He'd have to take a chance that his employers had just misplaced it on the map.

Making it across the street between a honking cab and squealing panel truck, Murphry reached the phone booth. He fumbled the door open and slipped inside. He glanced back the way he had come, but did not see the woman in black. Murphry forced the door shut and, avoiding the puddle of urine at his feet, crouched down to hide beneath the level of the scratched and greasy windows.

He grabbed the phone book dangling from its metal binder, and flipped it open at random, searching for a message from his employer. Surely they were watching him and knew he was in trouble. They would send him a message to try to help him out in this desperate situation.

Murphry tried the headers in the yellow pages, frantically flipping through the alphabet and tearing a few leaves, but found little meaning. He found "Body-Bookkeeping, Demolition-Dentist, Florist-Foot, Hardware-Health, Jewelry-Kitchen, Office-Oil and Martial-Massage." And though he conjured a world of meaning from each phrase, he was under too much stress to concentrate and determine how any of it might address his present situation and help him out.

The sudden scent of the woman in black coming through the door pushed away the smell of urine, oxidizing metal and concrete. Her smell was the smell of sex. Murphry's reservoir of suppressed memories sprung a leak. He put his hands to his head to stop the flow.

The woman was just outside the phone booth. He could see the shadow her head and neck cast upon the metal and glass wall he was facing. He placed his foot at the joint in the folding door to prevent her from opening it.

Murphry experienced a sudden chill, as if his ghost were crouched next to him. He felt he was going to die.

"Donny Dee," the woman said.

He didn't expect to recognize the voice. The memories were filling up his shoes, wicking up his pant legs.

"My mom calls me Donny Dee, but most everybody else calls me Donny," he explained to Leona.

"Your parents miss you and want to know if you're okay," the woman in black said. She must have gotten down on her knees and sent the words in through the crack in the phone booth door right at the level of his head. As chunks of masonry broke from the wall of the reservoir, recollections swirled around Murphry and he was having difficulty staying afloat in the present.

"Buddy, I don't know what to make of you sometimes," his father had said many times. He frequently addressed Donny Dee as Buddy, but his tone indicated that they would never be buddies. His father was a no-nonsense kind of guy, a construction contractor who'd been building low-income housing for the government for over twenty years.

Donny Dee knew he was not the son his father wanted. The young man was tall, just over six feet, but he was skinny and awkward. His thought processes had always followed unusual routes.

"Your mother has not been the same since you left," The woman in black continued. "She's not been well, but I know it would do her heart a lot of good if you were to come home to see her."

The wall of the reservoir gave way completely and Murphry found himself swimming in denied memories. He tumbled in the torrent and went under, awareness of the world around him totally eclipsed.

"It's just not natural for a boy your age to lose interest in television," Murphry's mother said one day. His father nodded in agreement, looking at his son with skepticism and suspicion in his eyes.

Both his parents allowed television to influence their social behavior, their eating and buying habits, even their political opinions, especially his mother. She seemed to take her cues from the characters in her soap opera and a few sitcoms. She watched the commercials intently as if they really had important information to offer her. Even so, she'd operate heavy machinery—her car—before finding out how a specific medicine would affect her. When he brought this to her attention, she'd point out that she was not on that medication. She complained that money was so tight she never could save any, but would rarely take the advice of commercials that told her how much money she'd save if she bought their products. There were some car commercials that offered to give you money if you bought their vehicles.

He didn't know why she didn't start a career of car buying. Perhaps it was because there wasn't enough room in the back yard to store more than a couple of cars, but why couldn't she just give them away? It was all very confusing.

Murphry was in his late teens before he realized that what he heard on television was often not the truth. He understood the difference between fiction and nonfiction when it came to drama, but commercials and the news occupied a gray area in his mind. Where he discovered the most apparent falsehoods was in advertising. Statements like, "We're here when you need us because we care" couldn't possibly be true. They didn't even know him. They were liars.

With time, he realized that nearly everyone accepted this type of communication as genuine, even his parents. He remembered his father saying once, "Of course I believe in free speech, but there are certain people expressing certain views the government shouldn't allow." It disturbed him to discover that most people spouted high ideals that they had no intention of respecting, and that nearly everyone expressed false concern in order to promote hidden agendas.

Why did he have to figure this out on his own? Why didn't his parents inform him? He would not find out the truth for some time to come.

"I come here t-t-t-to get away from m-m-m-my mom," Leona told him. "She works at n-n-n-nights and is no f-f-fun at all when she g-gets up to get ready for work. That's about the t-t-t-t-time I'm getting home from s-school. I come straight to the library from school to s-s-s-tudy. She doesn't care."

Donny Dee was reading a lot and hanging out at the library. That's where he met Leona. She was very well-read, intelligent, refreshingly straight-forward and honest.

"I come here to get away from the rest of the world," he said.

The first time they touched was an accident. Sitting together on one of the couches in the "comfy" room at the library, they had kicked their shoes off and were reading. Leona yawned, and when she stretched, her foot slid across the floor until it came to rest against his. Donny Dee thought she'd pull it away immediately, but she did not. Then he thought maybe he ought to pull his foot away, but he didn't want to. As simple as it was, that touch seemed very large in his mind. He couldn't continue his reading, though he pretended that he was. He risked a glance at her at just the moment she looked over at him nervously. She smiled.

Soon they were holding hands. Within the week, she had asked him to come back to her house after her mom had gone to work. They kissed and explored each other. Donny Dee ejaculated in his underwear and excused himself to clean up. When he came back Leona wanted to make love, but he couldn't get another erection. He didn't know shame could be so intense.

"It's okay, really," Leona said. "If I were m-m-m-more attractive—"

"It's not you, Leona. You're beautiful. It's—." How could he tell her he'd done it in his pants?

"Shhhh" she said, pulling him to her. They cuddled for a long while and then tried again. This time Donny Dee got an erection but somehow could not allow himself to ejaculate inside Leona. As far as he could tell, she didn't know the difference.

"I love you, Donny Dee," she said.

After high school, Donny Dee went to work for his father. His plan was to save up some money and go to college. He would study philosophy and ethics so he could teach them to preschool children. He didn't really like children very much, but thought they needed help understanding the world. This was a dream he kept to himself.

"Oh yeah..." the guy at the rental place said, "the hook that comes flying out of the sky to help you lift stuff. There's one hovering outside right now." Then he laughed. "Someone's making a fool of you, kid. Ain't no such thing as a sky hook."

It was his father's work crew that sent him to the rental place to get a "sky hook." They said they needed it to help move trusses into place.

The crew didn't like him. They became quiet whenever he approached unless he was the brunt of a joke.

Complaining that the lumberyard had sent boards too short, they sent him back to the shed to pick up a "board stretcher." He fell for that one too.

At lunch time, they drove him away and he sat and ate alone while hearing their derisive laughter in the distance. Until he learned to lock away his backpack, he'd find saw dust and nails in his food.

Gerald, an older crewman who didn't seem interested in mistreating Donny Dee, took him aside one afternoon. "Kid, the handwriting's on the wall," he said. "Why don't you quit before you get hurt? There's no shame in it. They treat you this way 'cause you're the boss's son."

Donny Dee shrugged this off, not understanding some of what Gerald was saying. Later he found the piece of sheet rock with the handwriting on it in a trash pile. It read, "Nutty as a fruitcake and dumber than a box of hammers." He thought he recognized the handwriting as belonging to one of the crew named Hank.

Donny Dee wrote a note to the man and slipped it into his lunch box. It read, "I've had fruitcake with very few nuts in it and it's dumb to think that hammers, in or out of a box, have any intelligence at all."

Later in the day, Hank grabbed Donny Dee by the shirt collar and said, "if I catch you getting into my lunch pail again, I'll break your arm."

Eventually their pranks were no longer jokes. Donny Dee had to be careful where he sat and what he picked up or he might find himself coated in sub-floor adhesive. He found deadly stinging insects in his backpack once and then they started poisoning his food. He stopped eating a midday meal.

His father thought he wasn't willing to get along with the crew.

When he told Leona about what happened on the job, she seemed skeptical. On one occasion she flatly refused to believe that one of the crew was keeping an eye on him through the scope of a high-powered rifle.

"Why don't you put down that newspaper and talk to us," Donny Dee's mom said.

He read the paper every morning at the breakfast table so he wouldn't have to talk to his parents.

Toward the bottom of page six he discovered an article about a young man and his problems with sex. Donny Dee recognized immediately that the article was talking about him.

He felt his temperature rising. His face was hot. His brain felt like it had flipped over inside his skull and his skin prickled from head to toe.

The article didn't come right out and say things plainly—more and more that was the way with even the newspaper these days—but you could read between the lines and understand it all clearly. Everyone would know about him. It listed in detail his sexual failures with Leona and attributed this to his masturbation technique involving the long, smooth handle of a particular hairbrush.

His parents—they were the only ones who could even possibly know about the hairbrush. Perhaps he didn't wash the handle well enough and his mom smelled it.

And Leona—she would have had to tell someone about their sex.

He lowered the paper. His parents were looking at him innocently.

"Why?" Donny Dee asked, tears streaming down his cheeks.

"Why what?" his father asked. "What are you blubbering about now?"

"Why would you do this? Why would you tell the world about me?"

"What are you talking about Donny Dee?" His Mother asked.

Donny Dee could see they were both going to play it innocent. He couldn't face them any longer. He grabbed his backpack and headed for the door.

As he exited, he heard his father calling after him, "You're expected to be on site in twenty minutes buddy."

"I didn't tell anybody anything about our sex!" Leona shouted at Donny Dee.

The librarian was hurrying in their direction, her forefinger pressed to her shushing lips.

This had not gone at all well. Leona was going to play it innocent also. But why?

The librarian, now within whispering range, said, "If you can't be quiet, I'm going to have to ask you to leave."

"Don't bother," Donny Dee said. He gave Leona one more sidelong glance, then grabbed his backpack and left the library.

"You're talking crazy talk, Donny Dee," his mother said when he called home. "Nobody is out to get you."

But Donny Dee knew different. He told her all about what was going on. He had reasoned that perhaps she didn't take part in having the article published. It just didn't seem like something she'd do. If anyone knew about the hairbrush, she'd be the one. She no doubt innocently mentioned it to his father. His father had done the rest. But how did he get the information out of Leona and why wouldn't she admit it?

Donny Dee couldn't go home. He couldn't go to work. Leona was at the library so he didn't want to go there. He wandered the streets thinking for a long, long time.

"Hey kid," came a voice from a blue car with *Sheriff* written on the side of it. The man driving the vehicle was wearing a plastic bonnet on his hat. He looked friendly enough. "You look hungry. What do you say I buy you a meal?"

Donny Dee was drenched from the rain and feeling miserable. He wasn't sure but thought he hadn't eaten in over twenty-four hours. He simply nodded his head and approached the car.

"The front seat is full of junk. Just get in the back."

The Sheriff seemed very friendly. Donny Dee assumed he would take him to a diner and they'd have a pleasant meal together. Maybe they'd become friends and then he'd have someone to protect him from some of the mean guys on his father's work crew. Maybe he'd find himself going out regularly for doughnuts and coffee with his new policeman friend. Donny Dee could ride along with him on his beat sometimes, help him reason out difficult cases he might be working on.

Instead of going to a diner, Donny Dee was taken downtown to the police station. On the way, the Sheriff explained that Donny Dee's father was an old friend from high school. "Said you were acting kinda strange and might need some help. He sent me looking for you."

Donny Dee didn't like hearing that. He felt a moment of panic, but was too tired to rise to its demands. When they got to the jail and the Sheriff directed him to enter a cell, Donny Dee resisted. "You can't put me in there."

Four policemen approached, filling up the space in the police station corridor.

"Look son, I owe it to your dad to hold you until he gets here. If you don't want to go with him, you don't have to. You're eighteen years old now, right?"

"Yes, just last week."

"So do me a favor and let's not make it difficult. While you wait, I'll get you a nice hot meal."

Donny Dee looked around at the other policemen without making eye contact with any of them. "Okay," he said.

"We couldn't get the emergency detention order," Donny Dee overheard his father say to the Sheriff, "but, Deke, you've got to help me out here."

"Without an EDO signed by Judge Fleece, I can't hold him any longer," the Sheriff said approaching Donny Dee's cell.

"The boy's sick," his father said. "He belongs in Central State Hospital."

Donny Dee was confused. He thought his father was trying to drive him away by shaming him the way he had, but now he wanted him locked up as well.

The cell door opened and Donny Dee looked his father squarely in the eyes. "You're the one that should be locked up."

His father's face turned angry and he grabbed for Donny Dee, but the Sheriff put his arm out to block him. "Son, if I were you, I'd go with your father, but it's up to you. You're free to go."

Donny Dee went straight to the bus station and left town, never to return. He had not seen his parents since.

He spent some tough years learning how to live on the street, wondering what to do with his life until the call came for him to join the ranks of Secret Policemen working for the True Government. Now thinking about what led up to him leaving home, he found answers for most of the questions left over from that period of his life.

Murphry understood why his parents didn't teach him to recognize the truth—they could not recognize it themselves because of the behavior modification program involving television. He knew that the False Government, those who controlled consumer society, was behind it. Their goal was to cloud each person's view of their own motivations by continually asking them to compare themselves to others. The resultant self-doubt a person experienced made them much easier to manipulate. He knew that the True Government tolerated the existence of the False Government for the same reason some organized crime protection rackets were tolerated by local police—with so few qualified persons to take on the mantle of the Secret Policeman, it filled a security vacuum. As long as the False Government's goals were limited to manipulating society for financial gain, the True Government would continue to tolerate them.

Murphry knew that his ability to think independently, a trait that made him invaluable to his current employer, made him a threat to those who ran the False Government.

He knew that the False Government had gotten their hooks into his father through his work—if he wanted to keep getting those big government contracts, he'd do their bidding. This was why his father tried to make him out to be insane so he could be put away in a mental institution.

He suspected that the Sheriff, although a friend of his father's, worked for the True Government just as Murphry did now, that perhaps he'd let Murphry go because he saw his potential and had informed his superiors that he might be a good candidate for Secret Policemanship. Maybe one day he'd meet up with him again and they would indeed go out for coffee and donuts and Murphry could thank him. It could be that they'd find themselves working on a case together, sharing clever banter as they chased criminals through the streets and across rooftops.

What he didn't know was how complicit his mother might have been in what his father tried to do and how Leona had been convinced to talk. Had she joined the False Government then or later?

"Why, Leona?" Murphry asked the woman in black through the phone booth door. "Why did you tell about our sex? Why did you join the enemy?"

On the wall, he could see her shadow stand up, shaking its head. "I still don't know what you're t-t-t-alking about," she said. "Look, I didn't mean to scare you. I think you were frightened when I showed you your old hair brush."

She was rapping lightly on the plastic window and Murphry turned to look. It *was* his old hair brush she was holding. It didn't look like a weapon anymore. How was she doing that?

"I asked your mom for something to help jog your memory," Leona said, pulling the door open a crack and speaking down at him. "She gave me this."

Murphry pressed himself against the back wall. "If you don't go away, I'll have to hurt you." His voice didn't have the power he'd hoped it would. And so he said it again, but this time the words only came out higher pitched.

She put the brush away. "Please, Donny Dee… I d-don't want to hurt *you*. I have been trying to f-find you for a long time. Five cities. A lot of libraries and… other… places. My cousin, Rebecca Anne, is the one who helped the most. When I told her I was looking for you, she said you were one of her clients. I was staying with her until we were in an accident and she drowned."

No wonder Miss Anne was turned. Her own family…, Murphry thought, consumed for the moment by the irony of it all. "You have put me in terrible danger."

"Yes…those policemen out front of the library…one day I hope you'll understand why I did that."

Murphry decided not to dignify that with a response.

"B-but are you okay?" she asked. "Are you safe and happy? You're living on the streets, aren't you?"

She knew how he lived. She'd been after him for months. *But perhaps she's two people now. She's the woman in black, the assassin sent by the False Government and she's Leona, the young woman who loves me.* If she was going to show concern, he could play along.

"You see how well dressed I am," he said, his voice still pitched too high. "Do I look like a homeless person?"

Leona didn't answer. The woman in black seemed far away while Leona was right next to him.

"I have a job and responsibilities. I eat three meals a day. I'm fine."

"I still love you."

What? She loves me? That's insane. She's a liar! "Maybe you do and maybe you don't, but if you do then you won't blow my cover. Now go away."

She bent a little closer. Murphry couldn't move farther back. His teeth clicked together protectively. "Don't you feel anything for me?" she asked.

"I won't love you. I can't love you. You have to go away."

There was a long pause.

"Okay, Donny Dee. I just had to s-speak to you. I had to see if you're okay. You're s-sure you're all right?"

"Yes!" In his ears it sounded like a roar, but the woman only shook her head as if it had been no more than a gentle request. Murphry squeezed his eyes shut and counted.

He counted to thirty-six, thirty-seven, thirty-eight. The woman in black was very far away, perhaps gone for good—Murphry could feel it. Then he heard Leona's footsteps retreating.

Even so, D.D. Murphry, Secret Policeman, didn't open his eyes until he reached one-hundred and sixty, and then waited for twenty minutes before exiting the phone booth.

Fragment: A Change of Heart

5:32 PM—Wednesday, May 3rd

"SPARE CHANGE?" THE MAN in the wheel chair asked D.D. Murphry, Secret Policeman.

Murphry saw him on the corner in his peripheral vision as he was walking by. "No thank you," he said. "I have plenty."

Then it struck him that he had perhaps misinterpreted what the man was asking. Murphry focused on the word "change." He saw an ad on the side of a nearby bus stop shelter that said, "Are you ready for a change?" The man in the ad was holding a cell phone and looking skyward.

There was one person in particular who'd made it his business to *change* Murphry.

He spun around quickly. Sure enough, the man in the wheel chair on the corner was Harold Posen. The man who wanted to be his "friend." Murphry had just escaped the clutches of a woman who "loved" him. He was certain it was all part of the same conspiracy to make him *care*.

And yet because Leona cared *so much about me, her alter ego, the woman in black, was thwarted in her attempt on my life, or worse!*

Harold seemed to recognize Murphry the moment he turned around. His eyes grew large and he dropped his cup of coins. Then he was reaching for Murphry, a smile on his face, his hands open and pleading.

This is my chance, Murphry thought. The left wheel of Posen's chair was poised on the sidewalk right next to the short drop off of the curb.

Murphry dashed behind Posen and grasped the handgrips of the wheel chair and turned him to face the traffic.

"How 'bout coffee," Posen said. "I know a nice place we can sit and have a cup and get to know each other."

He doesn't know I'm onto him—good!

The traffic was heavy, but moving swiftly. Murphry would shove Posen into an oncoming car, preferably a large one. He waited for such a car to come along, knowing that if he waited too long Posen might catch on to what he was doing.

"Actually, I don't drink coffee anymore," Posen said, "but this place I have in mind has a nice selection of teas."

There—a Lincoln Continental, a big, boxy coffin of a car, coming fast. That would certainly snuff the wretched fellow out. One big, heaving shove would do it. Murphry braced himself to put his weight behind the effort. He'd done this before. It wouldn't be hard… until afterward.

No wait—the guy driving the Continental looked like Shawn.

The wheelchair might come apart on impact, sending metal through the windshield to harm the driver. I've hurt Shawn enough already.

The next big car, Murphry told himself.

"I like bear claws or those big, fried apple-fritter-type things with my tea. What do you like?"

The burgundy Cadillac was coming even faster than the Lincoln. It was perfect until Murphry saw the woman driving. He told himself it wasn't his mother, but the resemblance was strong, and, of course, he hadn't seen her in several years—she might have changed. Even if the woman was a complete stranger, she was probably something like his mother.

And that's when he knew he couldn't do it—he couldn't destroy this evil representative of the False Government if it meant an innocent bystander might be hurt.

But why? What does this mean?

Murphry glanced around, worried that his employer had seen him hesitate. It was his duty to perform under any possible stress—to dispatch his enemy without a thought to the consequences.

Take action, now, he told himself, *before they* do *see.*

Murphry fumbled in his pocket for one of his air-filled syringes—he had a clear shot at Posen's carotid artery—but all he found in his coat pocket were his lollipops. He thought to remove his belt and strangle Posen, but knew that would take too long.

Murphry felt sweat trickle down the small of his back, though the afternoon was nice and cool. With his ambivalence, he felt his facial features twitch with confused expressions.

Is this cowardice? Where has my integrity gone? How have I come to such a sad state? What will Kate think if she finds out I could not perform my duty?

"You sure don't talk much, but that's okay. I'll do the talking for both of us if I have to." Posen chuckled. "I'm just glad you had a change of heart."

Murphry clutched at his chest, realization triggered by the man's words giving him a jolt like an electrical shock. He stumbled backward and Posen turned his chair around to face him.

"Are you all right?" he asked.

That's why I feel so different about people.

Murphry turned away and staggered down the block. He could hear Posen calling out to him, but soon his voice was lost in the traffic noise.

That's why I care. *But how did they get into my chest without me knowing about it?*

Mark My Words: Case #8

1:32 PM—Wednesday, May 10th

D.D. MURPHRY, SECRET POLICEMAN, was headed to Roosevelt Park, bearing a heavy emotional burden from recent events. He sprinted from one place of hiding to another to avoid being seen by satellite surveillance. As a dark cloud, evocative of his own mood, moved to blot out the sun, he dashed from under an awning at Cookie's Antique Emporium to the shade of a cherry tree at the edge of the Park and crouched beneath it, trying to make himself as small as possible.

In his mind, a powerful dread and a thin hope battled for supremacy. His worst fears told him he had utterly failed the True Government. He had now failed to dispatch two arch enemies. Would his employer cut him loose? *If they do, Kate will have nothing more to do with me. I will no longer exist for her. I am a complete washout, completely unlovable.*

Ever since becoming a Secret Policeman for the True Government, he had feared losing his position. And was his relationship with words contingent on his good relationship with the True Government? The two seemed to be linked. Without his *justification,* the messages he received through text made little sense, their meaning veiled and conveying only ominous, but incomplete warnings. He could not go back to the painful existence he'd had before, one with no purpose other than the daily struggle for survival on the streets. Looking back on that time in his life, he did not know how he had survived it.

But the worst result of losing his position with the True Government would be losing Kate. It seemed now just a matter of time.

Perhaps the right thing to do is to end it all before they suffer for my loss of integrity... and, of course, before Kate suffers. Surely their employer could annul their marriage before anyone else found out.

If I decide I must die, how should I go about accomplishing it? I don't want to suffer. Perhaps I could go to sleep with the intention of never waking up. What if I do awaken?

Murphry could think of no other method of suicide that wasn't frightening or painful. And he didn't really want to die. He wanted his old life back, but the False

Government had learned to penetrate his disguises quickly and were concentrating all their efforts on destroying him. Their goal was to change his mind. (Then he and Kate wouldn't even know each other!) He'd already had a change of heart. (Had this undone all his hard work to become lovable?) He didn't know how they might have achieved that, but the effects were obvious. His concern for those he'd accidentally harmed while fighting crime was overwhelming at times. It had played havoc with his decision-making.

Still Murphry clung to a thin ledge of hope. *Perhaps the True Government doesn't yet know of my deliquincies. It could be that even if they do, they are allowing me time to redeem myself and won't reveal my shame to Kate. If I can escape further notice by the False Government and have time to whip this new heart into shape, maybe my concern for the innocent might disappear for good and I can return to being an effective Secret Policeman.*

He tried to visualize Kate, but her image wouldn't form with any clarity in his mind. His pulse pounded in his neck and he bowed his head as tears spilled from his eyes. Wiping the wetness from his cheeks, he got up and moved quickly from one shade tree to another as he made his way through the park to his destination.

In the last week, Murphry had increased the frequency of his minor disguise changes and tried at least once an hour to make a major change, like temporarily wearing gloves, removing one shoe, wearing his jacket like an extra pair of pants. He'd made the mistake of plucking his eyebrows completely off, realizing that they were much harder to grow back quickly than other hair. Nevertheless, his efforts seemed to be working so far because the False Government hadn't caught up with him. That or the brain switch was much more difficult for them to pull off. All he could do now was to lay low and keep up the disguise shifts. For long term changes, he was concentrating on growing hair in his bald spot and had succeeded in shortening his arms by at least an inch.

He didn't know how much time he had. He was doing his best to expand that time with the power of his mind. Every day for a week now, he had come to the park with a book and sat for hours, trying to clear his thoughts and find a way to impress upon his new heart the sense of duty and purpose which had made his old one so heroic. He meditated on certain words and phrases, repeating them like a mantra—*honor...virtue...decency of language!.. rectitude...probity...high moral standards!.. integrity...promises kept!.. incorruptibility...duty fulfilled!*—hoping the intrinsic concepts would somehow recondition the weak emotional fibers of his heart. Today would be no different.

The sky remained cloudy, but still Murphry moved quickly toward his goal, a favorite tree. When he arrived, he spread his coat on the ground beneath it and sat with his back against the tree trunk.

He wiped the last, irritating tear from his face and then scoped out his surroundings. To his left were picnickers. To his right, a group of young men were throwing a Frisbee in the soccer field. A dog chased after the Frisbee, but never caught it.

He found himself scrutinizing the actions and words of a man who preached in the park. Murphry's tree was close to the park bench from which the preacher customarily delivered his sermons. He had seen the man many times over the course of the last year and heard him preach several times. Just recently he learned the man's name was Humewalter.

Now that Murphry was spending every day in the park, he realized that Mr. Humewalter preached here every afternoon. The preacher stood on the bench and, as if addressing a congregation, spoke to a seemingly empty lawn just south of the soccer field.

Murphry had always thought the man a nut who spoke to no one in particular. But recently, he began to experience some of Humewalter's belligerent religious attitude coming from others on the street. Now Murphry was convinced the preacher was the leader of a cult and that the sermons he gave in the park were provided for an invisible audience.

He tried to put it all out of his mind. *I need to lay low, concentrate only on my disguises and toughening up this new heart,* he told himself. *Integrity...promises kept!.. incorruptibility...duty fulfilled!.. honor...virtue...decency of language!.. rectitude... probity...high moral standards!..*

But why would they need to be invisible? Aside from upsetting everyone who doesn't believe as they do, what is the agenda and ultimate goal of Humewalter and his congregation?

Murphry knew of one homegrown terrorist organization the members of which wore sheets over their heads to remain anonymous. Invisibility worked even better. It even hid their numbers.

Humewalter's bunch don't even want to be seen going about their business. They must be up to something.

No, I must let it go. Perhaps I've even been sacked and no longer have any authority.

Rectitude...probity...high moral standards!.. integrety...promises kept!.. incoruptibilty...duty fulfilled!.. honor...virtue...decency of language!

Even so, if I perceived a clear and present danger from the congregation, I'm in a good position to do something about it. The question is: Will I have the guts—or should I say the heart—to do it? Perhaps this is a test?

His new heart gave no answer.

Murphry couldn't concentrate on his meditation. He dug out of his backpack a western novel and pretended to read it. An instant later, the Frisbee landed at his feet. As the dog ran to retrieve it, Murphy saw it dodging unseen obstacles. This was evidence that the preacher's congregation was gathering. Humewalter would soon arrive. Murphry was certain.

He allowed the dog to take the toy. A moan and an offensive "Oh shit" emerged from the group of frisbee throwers as the dog ran off into the bushes.

From those same bushes, Humewalter emerged moments later, wearing his stained overcoat and carrying the frisbee and his sandwich board. The dog didn't reappear.

Was the dog Humewalter? Murphry wondered. Was Humewalter the dog? Is Humewalter a dog?

He'd sort this out later.

Humewalter looked angry. His features were pinched up around his long, thin nose and his face was red all the way to the top of his bald pate. His white hair stood out from the sides of his head as if he'd been pulling at it.

Following the preacher was a thin, dark-haired young man who was clean-shaven except for a sprout of whiskers under his lower lip. Murphry had heard this referred to as a soul patch. The young man was carrying a backpack and wearing a stained T-shirt and very expensive pants, the kind that are worn out and have lots of holes in them. His face wore a sly grin. When he walked passed, Murphry saw the word Anarchy in large red letters on the back of his T-shirt.

A subversive! Murphry had an impulse to rise and beat the young man senseless, but if Humewalter's group was hooked up with such traitors, punishing the young man would reveal Murphry's surveillance.

Just keep an eye on him too.

The preacher tossed the Frisbee to the young men in the soccer field as he approach the park bench. Then he quickly spun around and lunged at the seditious punk. Laughing, Soul Patch danced out of the way.

"Care for a smoke?" the young man asked as Humewalter turned away.

The old man froze, then turned slowly back. Soul Patch pulled a pack of cigarettes out of his shirt pocket, shook one loose and offered it to Humewalter. As if reluctant to do so, the preacher took the cigarette, muttering a half-hearted, "Thanks."

Perhaps they are not in cahoots. I must wait and see.

Humewalter lit the cigarette. He donned his sandwich board sign, which read, "Read the Holy Bible," and stood on the park bench.

The young man sat cross-legged in the grass facing Humewalter about fifteen feet away from the bench. All smiles, he was devoting his attention to the old man.

Humewalter's only visible audience member.

The preacher cleared his throat loudly and then began shouting his sermon. "Teaching evolution in our schools does not square with God's intentions for us. Mark my words—in the time of reckoning, those who have invested in this Devil's theory will find they are spiritually bankrupt."

The phrase, "Mark my Words," was obviously a cue for the congregation to begin deciphering a code embedded in his sermon. But Murphy didn't have a high lighter or the text—probably a bible of some sort that no doubt each of the congregation possessed.

Murphry would have to be patient.

Yes, indeed, this is a test of my resolve. It is my next case, and it is the test which will determine if I—and my employer—can live with my new heart.

Where was his stress-relieving spoon when he needed it? He poked around in his leisure suit jacket pocket. There it was—it had slipped through a hole into the lining. He hadn't been aware this suit had a lining. None of his other leisure suits had one. He opened the jacket and looked inside, but couldn't see the lining. Just where was his hand going? Oh well, he had other pressing business at hand. He worked the spoon loose from the fabric and rubbed his thumb into it.

As Humewalter continued with his sermon, several of the picnickers and a pair of lovers in the nearby bushes gathered up their belongings and left the park. Now that the field was virtually empty of visible individuals, Murphry tried to assess the size of Humewalter's congregation. He counted depressions in the grassy field—spots where the grass was depressed under the weight of an invisible body—but there were so many, he lost track. This was disturbing. He had no idea there were so many members. He even saw depressions in the grass under nearby bushes. This meant there were so many that latecomers were forced to occupy uncomfortable spots.

The Anarchist is either a member of the congregation who has reasons for not being invisible or is merely a curious onlooker perhaps with no knowledge the congregation exists. Although he hasn't said anything, it's possible he's here to mock Humewalter.

"To accept that this perverted theory should be taught in our schools," Humewalter shouted, "is to aid the Devil in his seduction. Instead, we must become an irritant, a thorn in the side of a society that would allow any teaching that argued against the Holy Word of God."

He raised a copy of the Bible as he said this, and gave it a thump.

"Do you have to be such a cliché, old man?" Soul Patch said, giggling.

Humewalter let out a long wheezy sigh before continuing. "Yes, you will suffer as I do." He paused for dramatic effect and bowed his head and shook it slowly, then he raise his eyes to gaze past the reprobate to his congregation. There was fire in his eyes and a rumble in his voice as he said, "Those who do not do battle with the devil are not bedeviled. He will allow those who do not fight the good fight to have happy lives. They do his work and so he has no truck with them." After another dramatic pause, he added ominously, "Not in this life."

"Words," Soul Patch said. "So many words, old man."

The sneaky little bastard doesn't even value language. I will pay close attention to what he has to say.

And Humewalter—I'll just have to stick with him. Eventually, he'll let slip something that will lead me to the truth. But how—how do I stick with him without creating suspicion?

Humewalter's voice was cracking under the strain of his shouting. He dropped his cigarette butt and cleared his throat, coughing up a wad of phlegm and spitting it onto the sidewalk. "If you are not ostracized by all who do not share your beliefs, then you have not truly engaged the enemy."

"No wonder you are homeless and have no friends, old man," the anarchist said.

Soul Patch is obviously not part of the congregation and seems totally unaware of the many followers Humewalter has. If he pisses them off, they might act against him. I may not be able to defend him against an invisible force. I may not want to try.

"You should talk," Humewalter said, "a man over twenty years of age, still living with his mother."

Soul Patch shrugged, his smile unwavering. "You won't make many converts talking like that," he said.

"I may not be liked by many in this world," Humewalter said, "but I will have plenty of friends in the next."

If Humewalter pretends to be homeless, he's not likely to pass up the opportunity for a free meal. I'll offer to buy his lunch after the sermon. If he becomes suspicious, I'll pretend I liked what he had to say and am interested in hearing more.

Murphry, Humewalter and the anarchist, whose name turned out to be Ron Flackman, sat in a booth at the Treadwater Diner on Honeywood Boulevard having a late lunch. When Murphry had made the invitation to Humewalter, Flackman said, "I never pass up the chance for a free meal."

Murphry did not want to create unpleasantness while trying to keep track of the preacher so he just nodded his head. Besides, he had decided he needed to keep an eye on the anarchist as well.

On the way to the diner, Murphry learned a few things about the two men—they obviously spent a lot of time arguing with one another, they each had deep contempt for the other's beliefs and they both had something the other wanted.

Humewalter wanted Flackman's nearly inexhaustible supply of cigarettes. Every time Humewalter seemed to lose interest in talking with Flackman, the young man would offer the older one another smoke.

Flackman was an atheist and needed Humewalter's opposing opinion to argue against.

"It is generous of you to invite me to sup with you," Humewalter said to Murphry around a mouth full of meat loaf, mashed potatoes and green peas.

"You looked hungry," Murphry answered without looking at him. His two companions were in the habit of looking people in the eye when talking. Murphry knew better than to do this, especially when he was engaged in subterfuge. You never knew when you might meet up with someone who could see the truth behind your eyes.

Once all three men had finished the food on their plates, the preacher leaned back in his seat and let out a huge belch. Murphry knew that the other diners in the restaurant would be looking their way now, but he didn't look up from his plate.

He needed to figure a way to direct the conversation toward subjects that would help reveal what Humewalter's bunch were up to. But he had never been much of a conversationalist and developing that skill on the spot was giving him difficulty.

He reached for the spoon in his pocket and rubbed it. It calmed him enough that he thought of something to say. "Tell me… about who you hope to… reach," he said haltingly, "by preaching in the park."

"Are you a believer in our lord and savior, Jesus Christ," Humewalter asked, "or do you believe as young Ronny, here, that all in existence happened to arise from the void unbidden?"

That's not an answer to my question, Murphry wanted to say, but didn't. He bit his lower lip. He was reluctant to answer the preacher's question honestly for fear the man might lose interest in conversation. Still, he'd always felt that honesty was the best policy. Keeping his eyes focused on a smashed pea on his plate, he said, "No, but I believe in a philosophical sense in much of what he taught."

"Then I believe we don't have much to say to one another." He began to slide out of the booth, but Flackman was in his way.

"Leave the little fellow alone, Humus. He just bought you lunch and you have nothing but your backside to show to him?"

"We haven't had dessert yet," Murphry said.

The preacher settled back down. "A nice fellow like you and you don't believe?" he said.

Although he wished he had something to say, Murphry remained silent. His eyes searched the diner for text sources from which to receive messages or conversational inspiration, but this was made uncomfortable by his companions, occasionally catching his gaze. Almost all the text he found referred to food in some way and provided him nothing to work with. Finally he gave up looking for text and returned his eyes to his place setting.

"Of course he doesn't believe," the anarchist said. "He's a reasonable fellow."

He offered Humewalter a cigarette, but didn't offer one to Murphry. At that moment it dawned on Murphry that he had yet to see Flackman smoking. Did he smoke or were the cigarettes merely for Humewalter?

"It is outrageous to me that you to are an atheist," Humewalter said to Murphry.

"You assume he's an atheists," Flackman said, "because he doesn't believe what you believe?"

"There is nothing else," the preacher said curtly.

"If I asked you to believe in fairies," the anarchist said to Humewalter, "would you?"

"Why, of course not," Humewalter said. "Fairies are a myth and you know it. Their existence cannot be proven."

"That's the way I feel about your religion."

"Ahhh, but there are so many who believe as I do and for good reason."

"Safety in numbers, huh. Sounds like a mindless herd to me. No—wait… you guys refer to it as a flock. Sheep! Not a very flattering comparison. Do you know anything about sheep, Humus?"

Flackman followed this with a burst of laughter so loud it startled Murphry. Although he didn't look up, Murphry was certain the guffaw attracted the attention of everyone in the diner.

Humewalter was turning red again. His eyes narrowed and his brow furrowed. He raised an index finger and shook it in the air. "If what you believe is true, we'll never know, but if what I believe is correct we will both one day know the truth."

"Ooh… I'm quakin' in my boots here, old man. You really got me with that one. How long you been rehearsing that line anyway?" Flackman's giggles were manic and went on too long.

Humewalter was sliding out of the booth to leave again when he saw the waitress approaching. Without looking up, Murphry reminded him to order dessert and the preacher sat back down with a sigh. They ordered pie, apple for Humewalter, cherry for Murphry, rhubarb for Flackman.

"You know why I call the preacher Humus," Flackman asked Murphry.

Murphry shook his head.

"'Cause he's as cheerful as the grave!" Flackman laughed drunkenly, though Murphry hadn't seen him take a drink.

The waitress brought their desserts and they dug in.

When he was finished, Murphry caught Flackman's gaze with the slightest of glances, their eyes locked together for the briefest moment. "What... do you believe?" Murphry asked.

"I have no religious beliefs. I am an atheist."

"An atheist... believes there is no god. That is, uh... a belief."

"I cannot believe in that which I cannot see, taste, smell, hear or feel."

"There's no... evidence... either way."

"Hey, I've been around the block a few times. I know human nature. I—"

"You think he's... *foolish* to believe something he can't prove, but... *you* do the same thing."

Flackman was silent for a moment. He was as far from laughing as Murphry had seen him. Finally he said, "At least I don't expect anyone to believe as I do. But look what his bunch is doing—you watch the news, I suppose—they want more power in the courts over issues like abortion, assisted suicide and what's taught in schools. Extremist Christians think they represent the majority. Assuming all Christians believe the same way, they think judges are not adhering to the will of God and so are not adhering to the will of the people. They want to change the law of the land to reflect their beliefs."

Now there was anger in Flackman's eyes. "Tonight there's a school board meeting at the main library. There's a new extremist Christian member on the board who's trying to get passed resolutions for new teaching standards and curriculum that will sideline the teaching of evolution and replace it with something called 'Intelligent Design.' You know—the teaching that God created the Earth in seven days and all that shit. There are currently efforts to censor certain books in the library. Some science books have already been destroyed and they're not being replaced."

Humewalter nodded his head in evident approval.

"If they don't get their way," Flackman said, dire warning in his voice, "there's no telling what they'll do."

There was a smug smile on Humewalter's face. "We'll do whatever we have to—bomb the place if need be." The smile left his face suddenly, as if he knew he'd gone too far.

A confused set of emotions flickered across Flackman's face.

Did the old man just reveal his congregation's plot?

"I've got the Lord's work to do," Humewalter said, shoving the anarchist out of the way and exiting the booth and the restaurant in a hurry.

Flackman pulled the pack of cigarettes out of his pocket as he chased after him.

Murphry was left to take care of the check.

Denouement—Of the Same Mind: Case #8 Continued

3:47 PM—Wednesday, May 10th

*H*UMEWALTER IS GOING TO *bomb the library! He and his invisible congregation are going to blow up the building where my precious Kate works! And not only will she be there, but so will hundreds of other innocent citizens who are merely interested in the best education for their children!*

Murphry made his way back to Roosevelt Park—shoving along the streets while trying to stay unobtrusive to pedestrians—hoping to find Humewalter back in his preaching place. He needed to follow the man's every footstep to prevent this dreadful plan from taking place.

But Humewalter was not in the park, and the fact that people were playing touch football in the field his congregation had occupied told Murphry that the preacher's followers were not there, either.

Murphry's hands clenched into fists and out again, in and out. He dropped down onto the very edge of the bench that served as the preacher's pulpit to gather his wits. Could he gain enough control over his new internal organ to do what had to be done? Had his meditations reconditioned it at all? He'd been able to disguise himself with the eyebrows, the bald patch, and the shorter arms, but Humewalter had just spent more than an hour sitting across from him at the restaurant, so the disguise would no longer fool him. Murphry concentrated. He needed to make additional changes. *Think, think, think.* There. His arms were back to their original lengths. His hair was three shades lighter. He hoped that would be enough to fool Humewalter.

He grappled the paperback novel from his pocket and flipped through it. No words rose from the pages to rescue him. *Damn and double damn!* he thought without regret. He shoved it back down into his jacket. Across the stretch of green, a trash truck backed up to a steel Dumpster, slid its lifting bars into place along the sides of the trash receptacle, raised the metal box up and over the cab and dashed the contents into the bowels of the truck. The sign on the truck's side read, "Keep Our City Clean! Put Trash Where it Belongs!"

Murphry felt his heart flutter. This meant something. The True Government was sending this message. If they were aware of his deliquincies, they had decided to give him another chance.

He scribbled on the back of a business card, "Put Trash Where it Belongs!"

Now to get to the library and stop the insane preacher before anything could happen. It was just a matter of a few hours until the meeting.

I will have to head him off at the pass. I will have to risk my own life to save that of the others. The True Government is indeed testing me. If I succeed, it will be the proof they need that I can still be trusted.

He sat across from the library in the bus stop shelter as the sun went down and the crowds began to show up. No doubt many were members of Humewalter's congregation, but how would anyone know for certain? *How clever Humewalter and his crowd have been.*

Murphry had gone through an entire copy of a discarded Sports Illustrated Magazine he'd found on the bus, page by page, searching for clues, determined to eat any page that offered information so only he could know it, and know it from the inside out. But there was nothing in the magazine of any value, not a single helpful phrase or term. And so, he shredded the pages one by one, and put them into the receptacle near the bus stop sign.

I need more information! I need more help! How will I save Kate and the others if I don't have more information? But more information was not forthcoming. More help did not step forward.

First the small parking lot to the left of the library filled up with mini vans, SUVs, and sedans, then the parking spaces along the street. Murphry watched each and every person who went up the front steps and into the library. Parents with children. Grandparents with children. Women who looked like teachers. Women and men who looked like preachers. Some carried signs. Others wore ribbons. *Any of them could be one of Humewalter's bunch. Any of them might be carrying a bomb.*

The topic tonight is drawing them out like flies. Where is Humewalter?

More cars, more people. Where would they fit them all? They would have to stand up inside, that was for certain.

More cars, more people.

Where is Humewalter? Maybe he's changed his mind or maybe his mind has been changed.

And then, at five minutes until seven, Humewalter came striding up the sidewalk on the library's side of the street. He wore a bulky coat, wrapped around and belted. His head was bent low, as if he were carrying a heavy burden.

It is Humewalter who has the bomb. His ego would not allow anyone else to do the job. His followers are just running interference for him tonight.

Murphry stood. He ran across the street and got into the crowd just two people behind the crazed preacher. They moved up the steps. Murphry squeezed through shoulders and elbows, and took Humewalter by the arm. Humewalter spun about, nearly knocking a young woman down as he did, and he looked at Murphry with befuddlement. *Good, the disguise is working.*

"Can we talk?" Murphry asked.

"About what?" Humewalter said, jerking out of Murphry's grasp as more people pushed up and around them. "There is important business going on inside. The Lord's business!"

"Come out to the street for just a moment," Murphry said. "Tell me about the Lord's business. I want to hear what you have to say."

"Puh!" Humewalter said. That was all. Just "puh!" Then he stormed up the stairs and into the library.

I can't let on about him, I can't let on about me! Murphry thought. *I have to just get him out of there! I'll write a note, let words trick him and lure him out. It can say, "God wants to talk to you! Right now! Back at Roosevelt Park!"*

Murphry reached the front door. Oliver Ingram stood there, and when he saw Murphry, he snarled, "You can't come in here. This is a forum of the school board. Now, go!"

"A public forum," said Murphry. "Open to the public, the sign outside says so."

"Sir, don't make a scene. Just go, quietly, please."

"It's open to the public, the sign says…"

Another man Murphry didn't know said, "Folks, the building has reached its capacity. The Fire Marshall will not allow any more."

Those behind Murphry were turning away with some grumbling.

Murphry remained. "But—" he began, then tried to quickly bull his way in.

Oliver, with surprising strength for an older man, and another man, snatched Murphry up by the shoulders and forced him back down the steps to the sidewalk.

The man Murphry didn't know said, "We were asked to make sure the meeting is orderly. Sir. I'm sure you understand our need to keep things orderly."

"It's open to the public, the sign says…"

And then the man gave Murphry a shove. Not a big shove, not enough to knock him down, but enough to let him know that he was in charge and Murphry was not getting inside.

Murphry stared up the steps as the big front entrance door was drawn shut.

There had to be a back door to the library. And, it was probably locked. It was worth a moment to check, however. Maybe someone, a janitor, high school volunteer, left it open so he could go in and out for a smoke without hauling keys with him. Murphry skirted the building out of the eyeshot of Oliver-on-the-steps, through the parking lot, and around to the back of the big, stone building. He thought briefly on how many back entrances he'd been forced to use in his lifetime. Something to ponder later, maybe. Maybe it meant something. Maybe it didn't.

There was a single Dumpster there beside the rear door. No window glass to shatter in this one. And there was Flackman. Soul Patch. Standing with a crowbar and a hammer by that same door, in his expensive pants, his pack slung over his back.

"Hey, oh, shit, ya caught me!" Flackman said. "Wait, I know you! What are you doing here, my man?" He winked his eye at Murphry.

He can't know me. I'm disguised.

"They wouldn't let me come in," said Flackman. He was clearly drunk, or high on something. "Bastards! Wouldn't let you in either?"

"What are you doing?"

"Just exercising my rights as a citizen," he said. "Letting myself in. Want to join me?"

"Well, yes." *Good, I can get in and find Humewalter! I hope I'm not too late.*

Flackman wedged the crowbar into the crack between the door and its frame and whacked it with the hammer. It gave a little but not enough. "Fuck, man," said Flackman. Then he whacked again. Still, just another dent. "Fuck, fuck, fuck, fuck!" The next few whacks missed their marks, but then he landed one solid enough to drive the crowbar through. With gritted teeth, Flackman worked it back and forth and back and forth until it came open with a scrape and a pop.

"I'm in a hurry, my man!" Flackman said to Murphry as the two went inside. "Countdown to a glory hallelujah! Can't miss this!"

"No, can't miss this," said Murphry. They were in a hallway, with storage rooms and small meeting rooms to either side. On the wall were posters advertising the newest children's books, decorated with colorful, wall-eyed animals and balloon-headed people. Up ahead were steps that led to the first floor.

Flackman trotted toward the steps, with Murphry on his heels. He giggled like a girl. It was very strange. He seemed more than drunk. He seemed totally elated.

The door to the right of the steps opened. Kate came out, with several books in her hands. She stopped and stared. She looked truly shocked to see the two there. Her bun wobbled on her head.

"What are you two doing?" she said in her best angry voice, though he detected a trace of fear.

"Kate," said Murphry, "I… I want to attend the meeting. They wouldn't let me in the front."

"So, I let him come in with me," said Flackman, flipping the crowbar cheerfully in his hand as if it were a baton. "What an idiot! A lamb to slaughter is what I'd say. But what's one dead homeless dude among, what, one hundred? Two hundred? That would be my guess."

"What are you saying?" Kate insisted.

"I don't have time for this. Get out of my way, you big, fat slob," Flackman said.

"What?" wailed Kate.

Flackman lifted the crowbar and swung at Kate. She raised her arms to defend herself, but the blow sent her crashing to the floor in a blur of books, bun, and voluptuous beauty.

No! thought Murphry. *No no no no no!* He felt the power of his job rise up in him, the power of the words and wisdom of his meditation fill his new heart, the power of righteousness and knowledge fill his brain and quickly boil up in him until he felt he would burst. Flackman stood over Kate, preparing to bash in her brain… the brain that had never been picked. Driven by the unsummoned but delicious energy, he dove for Flackman like a lineman dives for a ball (he thought linemen dove for balls though he couldn't really be sure) and caught the man around the waist. Kate rolled out from under as they hit the floor in a tangle.

Flackman got away from Murphry and then they were both on their feet again. "If those religious nuts don't get their way," he said, "there's no telling what they'll do. I'm going to nip it in the big fat, godly-ass bud!" Flackman grinned, then raised the crowbar at Murphry. "Time's a-wastin', retard!" The crowbar whistled through the air, arching down toward Murphry's head, but he ducked out of the way, surprising himself with his speed as he'd never had to jump out of the way of a crowbar before. The bar grazed his shoulder, cutting the shirt and gouging the flesh.

Murphry leapt and tackled Flackman again. The crowbar flew from the anarchist's grasp. Then the Secret Policeman hopped up, grabbed the flailing, furious kid by the heels and dragged him back down the hall. It was easier than Murphry could have imagined or hoped for. He felt almost… superhuman.

"Wait, man, you believe the same as I do!" shouted Flackman, his eyes wide and white, struggling like a trout snagged on a wire. "The bomb…in my backpack… we've only got about a minute!"

"What?" said Murphry. *He's going to blow the place up? I thought Humewalter was going to do that.*

"I didn't really mean you're a retard! I was kidding! We're of the same mind! I knew that the minute we had lunch today! Let me go! I've got to get up to that conference room. We can do this together!"

"Shut up, Soul Patch." Murphry pulled Flackman out over the doorsill and out to the Dumpster—the kid cracked his head on the sharp metal edge and whined—and then Murphry knew what his earlier message had meant.

The words told me all I needed to know, Murphry thought. *Put trash where it belongs.*

Murphry kicked the struggling Flackman in the head so he would stop struggling, then tossed back the heavy lid of the trash receptacle. With three deep breaths and a couple loud grunts, he hoisted the kid and the pack over and into the can. He slammed the lid back down. Then he ran for the library door, just making it back into the hallway when the Dumpster blew.

And blow mightily, it did.

With the roar of metallic thunder, Flackman, his message, the Dumpster, and lots of library trash went heavenward and side-wards. Shards and bits of flesh flew into the hallway, barely missing Murphry, who dropped against the wall with his hands over his head and his eyes squeezed shut. The smell that followed was hot and acrid.

Murphry waited. He waited. He waited. It seemed like a long time, but that was okay. Then he opened his eyes.

Smoke and dust hung heavily in the air. Murphry, disoriented, stumbled down the hall in what he hoped was the right direction. But then his foot caught the bottom of the steps and he fell forward. As the air cleared, he looked up to see a rash of school board members, silent for a brief moment, and staring. But then the silence broke suddenly and they rushed down the stairs to greet and thank him. One rather large woman hugged him and pounded him on the back. In a panic, Murphry turned around to escape, to get out of the library, but bumped into someone standing in his path.

It was Kate. Murphry had never had such contact with her. He gained a nearly instantaneous erection.

Kate leaned forward and gave him a kiss on the forehead. "Thank you," she said, lightly gripping his left upper arm. He could feel the warmth of her hand spreading down his arm and up his shoulder, across his chest, carrying with it a thrill of touch unlike anything he'd felt before. He had never dreamed he could feel so connected to another person by such a simple gesture. And the look of adoration in her eyes!

"You saved us all," she said.

If he were to die right now, he would do so happy and fulfilled. But he wasn't going to die!

Murphry wanted to grab Kate and take her to the floor where they would have glorious sex, but he remembered they were not alone. The board members continued to slap him on the back and congratulate him for an amazing and heroic job. Murphry kept his eyes on Kate. He didn't want to face the Board members. The attention was awful! He knew they would expect him to say something, but he didn't want to.

Then he remembered the suckers in his pocket and the reason he'd bought them. Here was his chance. He turned and tossed a handful of the lollipops at the Board members, thinking they'd scramble after them and he and Kate would be able to make their escape gracefully. But as the candy showered down on the five men and four women, they seemed merely confused for a moment and then they resumed expressing their thanks in a muddled overlapping of words.

A loud voice rose above the din. "Is this the gentleman who stopped the bombing?"

Murphry whirled around to see a uniformed policeman standing next to Kate, another three official-looking men in dark clothes and four more police officers had entered the room and were spreading out.

"Yes, officer," Kate said. "He's our hero."

No—she knew better than to tell him that! Murphry was horrified.

Of course they would have called the police—why didn't I think of that and make my escape earlier?

He knew it was because he had allowed himself to be overwhelmed and distracted by the reaction of his lovely wife. *That bad heart of mine again. The reconditioning was incomplete!* And now she was nodding her head and squeezing his arm gently. Obviously she could read the panic on his face. "It's all right," she said. "You did a good thing."

But Murphry was frightened. He was surrounded by members of the False Government! If he and Kate were identified at this moment—the happiest moment of their married lives—it was the end for both of them.

A middle-aged man in a black overcoat and felt hat came into the room, barking orders at the other officers. He spoke with one of the uniformed officers for a moment, then the policeman pointed in Murphry's direction. The man in the overcoat and hat took one look at Murphry and moved straight for him, realization clearly dawning on him.

Murphry quickly turned his eyes away, looking down. Black pits seemed to open in the floor at his feet and his legs felt unsteady. He could not focus on any ideas for getting out of this mess.

It wasn't his fault. It was the damned heart! *I should have ended it all a week ago. Then Kate would not have to suffer as well.* His gut sank into one of the pits at his feet.

"Are you Donny Dee Murphry?" the man asked.

Murphry didn't want to look at him, but he raised his eyes, and, suddenly, everything changed—he recognized his father's high school buddy, Deke, the sheriff who'd helped him escape from his father and no doubt arranged for the True Government to hire him. This was all an act for the benefit of the other officers, those of the False Government who were watching. Deke would have everything under control, Murphry was sure. He knew he could trust him.

The pits in the floor closed up. Murphry smiled, nodded his head and said, "Yes, I am." He was certain he'd be given a new name later.

"Isn't that something," Deke said, "you being the one to stop this bomb plot? Well…" He shook his head, a look of wonderment on his face.

There was an awkward silence as the two men stared at each other and then Deke seemed to catch himself. "And you, you're probably wondering about me. I work for the city now. Moved over here—what… just about two months ago."

Murphry leaned forward so that only Deke could hear him and said, "Can you get us out of here?" He gestured toward Kate.

"We'll need to get statements from everyone who saw the suspect."

"You mean you want to debrief us?" Murphry asked.

"Yeah…" Deke said as if he didn't know how to respond to this, "something like that." He turned to Kate. "Did you see him too, Ma'am?"

"Yes, sir," Kate said. "He's been coming to the branch now for a few weeks. I had become suspicious, but I never suspected anything like this!"

Deke turned to one of the plain-clothes officers, who was talking to the board members and other library staff. "If you've got this under control, " he said, "I'll take these two with me." The man nodded his head.

"Okay then, you two, let's go." Deke led Murphry and Kate out of the library to a black car with a whirling blue light on top. Deke opened the back seat door and Kate and Murphry got in. He got in the front, started the car and pulled away from the curb and into traffic.

While Murphry was thrilled to be riding in a car with Kate, he had a nagging suspicion that all was not right. Of course her presence and calm should have been enough to reassure him. Deke had done him no harm in the past and had perhaps helped him into the position that had made his life worth living. He looked over at Kate and she smiled warmly. Still…

He wanted reassurance, maybe advice from his employer, but the words he saw through the windows were street and traffic signs and gave him nothing. He looked around the inside of the car for text sources, but found none. This was strangely reassuring to him as he realized that a True Government employee such as Deke would not have any permanent forms of documentation in his work area. Still…

Murphry wanted out. It was all he could do to keep himself from opening the car door and leaping out as they approached the police station. They were going into the lion's den and he knew he must show no fear lest he give himself away.

But why would they go there? Was it that this Police Station of the False Government was the last place his enemies would think to look for him? Was there such wisdom involved in the decision to go there? He opened his mouth to ask these questions, but stopped himself.

No, I must not let my sweet Kate and Deke see that I have become a coward by asking a lot of questions. I will not let this flawed heart get the better of me in this finest of all possible moments.

At the station, he screwed up his courage and got out of the car, then bit his lip to keep the questions in and followed Deke and Kate into the building.

The signs around the metal detector asked him to remove his shoes, belt and any metal objects from his pockets. He found he could not reinterpret the instructions. Following Deke's and Kate's example, he placed his shoes, belt and his key ring in a plastic tub. His spoon seemed to have slipped into the nonexistent lining of his jacket again and he couldn't work it loose. He gave up on it and stepped through the metal detector, hoping the spoon wouldn't set it off and draw attention to him and was relieved when it did not. Deke offered Murphry the plastic tub so he could retrieve his belongings and Murphry sat with the others to don his shoes.

While he was below eye level, he glanced about the room for text sources.

His eyes lit upon a sign that said "The Miranda Warning" in large type at the top, then continued beneath that in smaller type, "You have the right to remain silent.

Anything you say may be used against you in a court of law. You have the right to consult an attorney before speaking to the police and to have an attorney present during questioning. If you cannot afford an attorney, one will be provided for you at government expense."

An expensive present, Murphry thought, knowing something about what attorneys cost.

He knew the sign was for the criminals brought here under arrest, but it also contained a message for him. He was to remain silent because the False Government could hear everything he said while in this building.

He kept his eyes focused on the floor tiles as they negotiated several corridors. Murphry saw the legs of those he could only assume were members of the False Government. He knew they were watching him.

Finally Deke stopped and gestured for Kate to enter a small room. "We'll be in the room next door," he told Murphry.

Murphry wanted to speak up in protest, but he slapped his hand over his mouth to prevent the words from emerging. His panic was apparently obvious, however.

"It's all right, really," Kate said, smiling to reassure him. "Don't worry." She entered the room and Deke shut the door.

Murphry followed him down the hall a short way and into the next room. Inside, he saw a large window-like mirror in the wall between this room and the one Kate had entered. There was a table in the middle of the room with a chair on either side of it.

Murphry's ears were hot. His mouth had dried up. Something was wrong with this situation. There were no text sources within reach from which he might seek advice.

Deke gestured for him to take a seat. As he cautiously sat down, Murphry saw another table against the far wall with items stacked on it: a file folder filled with various documents, a clip board like the one he'd taken from Harold Posen, an ad for a furniture store with burn marks along one edge and the bent fender of a scooter like the one Murphry had used for a time. There was his battery-operated can opener and an envelope with the name, Robin, in large block letters—his handwriting. Then he recognized his stress-reliever spoon. It was mounted on a piece of wood, almost as if it were prepared as evidence. He thought he had long ago rubbed the bloodstains off of it, but even from a distance, he could clearly make them out.

A chill ran up his spine and suddenly his faulty heart was racing and he broke out in a sweat.

How did they assemble all that stuff? Murphry knew where some of it was supposed to be—mementos of some of his cases he kept in an old WWII ammunition box stored in a locker at the bus station—but how had they gotten their hands on the rest of it, the fender of the scooter, the biology magazine missing its crossword puzzle and the Bible that was stolen from him over a year ago?

Sweat trickled down his forehead and dripped from the end of his nose. He kept glancing up at the big mirror-window, wondering what or who might be on the other side.

Deke seemed to catch this. "Don't worry, this is just between you and me for now." He pulled a notebook out of the inside pocket of his jacket.

Kate also had said, "Don't worry." *Do they think I'm an idiot?*

Murphry knew what he was in for, but how had it all come about?

Did the False Government change Deke's mind and *Kate's?*

Was she now a totally different person from whom she had been, lost to him forever? If so, all was lost; his job, his relationship with words and his wife. If everything had been an act on her part, then she had never actually come close to loving him. The thought of it all was dizzying and much too real. And at this moment *everything* was too real—the objects and textures in the room crystal clear, the air sharp in his lungs, the sounds crisp on the edges, his thoughts, like monuments, static and permanently fixed in his mind—inescapable.

And then the room and everything in it seemed to be receding, going soft on the edges.

"Your father had good reason for wanting you off the street," he heard Deke say, but his words were fading in intensity and sounded as if they were coming from a great distance. "We knew you needed help, but you were on the move so much it was difficult to track you down. Of course your activities are well documented now. We knew you were getting into a lot of trouble. Now that we've finally brought you in, everything will be different."

Murphry's breathing stopped. His heart paused in mid-beat. *Is this it?* he wondered, his head swimming with regret. *Am I going to sleep now with the intention of never awakening?* The blood drained from his brain and his vision dimmed, blackness creeping into his peripheral vision.

Then Deke was propping him up and gently shaking him by the shoulders. "Are you all right?" he asked. "The excitement is too much for you, isn't it?"

Murphry sat up in his chair. His heart was beating again, his chest was rising and falling and his vision had returned to normal.

Deke moved to the table against the wall and picked up the piece of wood the spoon had been mounted on. "We didn't know what to do for you. This was a last minute thing really." He held the mounted spoon up for Murphry to see.

Now that he could see it clearly, Murphry saw that the wood was actually a plaque of sorts and beneath where the spoon was mounted to it, there was a brass plate with words etched into it that read, "In recognition of his selfless sacrifice and service above and beyond the call of duty in the face of insurmountable odds, this honor is conferred upon Donny Dee Murphry by an agency that shall not be named."

Murphry squinted, trying to rearrange the words, looking for more meaning, but it seemed to be a message meant simply to honor him. Speechless, he stared at it unbelieving for a moment.

Deke showed him a huge smile. "Like I said, it was a last minute thing. You can't even take it with you. We'll have to destroy it, but we wanted you to see it. We wanted you to know how much your efforts are appreciated and that we know that it hasn't been easy for you to live the way you have in order to perform your duty."

Was this a trick? Murphry had been certain that he was about to be slapped in irons and thrown into a deep, dark hole to be tortured for information about his involvement with the True Government. His counterfeit heart didn't know what to do. It skipped a beat or two, then ran forward at an accelerated pace. Where a moment ago, his thoughts were immovable object, now they had wings and could not be pinned down.

Deke—

The False Government—

And words, his life, his job—

Kate, his lovely wife who loved him—

His heart had not gotten the better of him. He had survived in spite of everything.

And… he, Murphry, was being honored for his service! He'd never thought this possible.

Am I worthy of it?

He didn't have a chance to think about that. The mirror-window became clear and he could see Kate and several of the other officers in the room next door. Some of the officers were throwing confetti. Kate had shed her disguise, the hip pads, the pendulous breasts, the dewlaps from her neck and the backs of her arms. She had let her hair down and it fell about her shoulders, a gorgeous golden-red. She wore a stunning green satin evening gown, and she was holding a champagne flute. One of officers was refilling it with more champagne. She giggled lightly at the bubbles.

"We are providing you and Kate an all-expenses-paid vacation for a month at the Cha-Cha Paradise Resort on beautiful Copacabana Island."

Now Murphry could hear laughter from the other room, from Kate and the officers, coming through speakers set high in the wall above the mirror-window. Then a Barry Manilow song started up and they began to dance, Kate beckoning to him with hula-dancer-like gestures.

Deke set the spoon-plaque down on the table and offered his hand to Murphry. "Would you like to go and join the celebration? It is all for you. We have cake and champagne, and then when you're ready, a stretch limo will take you two to the airport."

Murphry placed his hand in Deke's and allowed the man to help him to stand. Was that the shakes that made him quake so or had the rhythm of the song and the moment gotten into him? Though he was unsteady on his feet, he almost felt as if he could dance, and more, that he could do it in front of Kate and the others!

Ah, yes!

"When you get back from your vacation, I was hoping you'd team up with me on some special high-risk duty. It'll take a Secret Policeman with your experience and tenacity to help bring to justice the scum bags we've been after. I've wanted you in my unit for a while now, but knew you needed to complete some important operations."

I'll have a partner, a confidant, a…. friend!

And Kate knows how special I am! At last I am truly and completely loved!

He looked back at the spoon-plaque, as if that might reassure him that this was all real.

"You'll have to leave that here, you understand."

Murphry nodded his head and stuck his hands into his jacket pockets to hide his trembling. His right hand closed on his stress-reliever and he began to rub his thumb into it.

Wait a minute—how can the spoon be mounted on the plaque and be in my pocket at the same time?

"Are you coming?" Deke asked.

Which of them is the real spoon?

D.D. Murphry, Secret Policeman, pulled the spoon out of his pocket and left it on the table before exiting the room.

Afterword

BETH MASSIE, HER SISTER, Barbara Spilman Lawson, and I developed D.D. Murphry, Secret Policeman, during the hours we spent together in a van traveling from Rhode Island to Virginia. I know the trip took many hours, but it zipped by as we talked about Mr. Murphry and his unique perspectives; and as we imagined situations to put him in and *discovered* his outrageous reactions and responses to these hypotheticals. We cut a path of imagination and humor through seven States, our laughter scattered in our wake for hundreds of miles.

Of course we resolved to write a story about the Secret Policeman, but none of us took up the task for many years.

But Murphry would not go away. Every time I saw a homeless man wearing something hopelessly out of style, but holding his head up in an effort to maintain dignity, I thought of Murphry. I thought of him whenever I misread something and received from it a bizarre, humorous or off-the-wall message—something I refer to as *creative misunderstanding.*

The world is much more surreal when taken literally. I remember shopping at a grocery store that had labels in its frozen food bins to indicate what you'd find in each section. One was *Battered Chicken Parts*. It was of course a section containing chicken parts dipped in batter for making fried chicken, but the Secret Policeman in me took a totally different meaning from the words.

I thought of D.D. Murphry while I was doing a demonstration of spontaneous painting techniques at a book store in San Francisco and a homeless man told me he saw faces in the paint I was pushing around with a rag. "That's why I push the paint around with rags, tin foil and plastic," I told him. "It makes impressions in the paint and I can look into the shapes created and find forms to bring out. Sometimes they're faces, sometimes I see other things."

He leaned in close and whispered to me, "So you see 'em too, huh?" He told me about the faces of famous people he had seen in the linoleum floor of a kitchen. "I know they were put there by human design," he said, "but no one believed me."

He watched me for a while as I found and brought out figures and faces in the painting I was developing.

"You see 'em too," he said after a time. Seemingly comforted by this notion, he left the store.

This incident really got me thinking about Murphry and finally I could resist the Secret Policeman no longer. I wrote "His Grandmother's Eyes," "Under My Skin" and "Change Your Mind," as short stories.

Then Beth and I discussed turning it into a novel. Now Murphry could not be contained. We developed plot elements that were recurring and transitioning themes, including an emotional change in the Secret Policeman, to create an over-arching story line for the novel.

Beth wrote "An Arm and a Leg," "Head on a Platter" and "Picking Her Brain."

I added "The Handwriting on the Wall" and "Pull the Wool Over His Eyes" to help give Murphry a history, and the fragments, "Eat My Words," "Friends Like These," "A Gag Gift" and "Change of Heart."

We collaborated on the last two chapters, "Mark My Words" and "Of the Same Mind."

For me, the tough part of writing this material was that for each episode two stories had to be told; the one based on Murphry's assumptions and the one the audience would read between the lines. The easy part came from Murphry's ability to rationalize and justify. The storytelling territory this presented was vast and uncharted. The possibilities were endless.

D.D. Murphry, Secret Policeman, causes a lot of pain and suffering—as writers of dark fiction, Beth and I had a lot of fun with that—but if we sympathize with him, it is because we see that his motives are good. That obviously doesn't excuse him of his crimes. Sorry, Murphry, but actions *do* speak louder than words.

Even so, it is good to keep in mind that everyone's perception is flawed and that there are times for each of us when self doubt clouds our thinking and it is difficult to determine what is real. When this happens, it helps to remember that what really matters is what motivates us. If we can be clear about our own motives, we don't have to be concerned about what others think of us.

Somehow I know that D.D. Murphry, Secret Policeman, is not done with me. I do hope he considers me an ally.

—Alan M. Clark
Eugene, Oregon

About the Authors

Alan M. Clark

Alan M. Clark grew up in Tennessee. He is most known for his work in illustration, which appears in books of fiction, non-fiction, textbooks, young adult fiction and children's books. His awards in the illustration field include, the World Fantasy Award and four Chesley Awards. His fiction has appeared in magazines, anthologies and a collection released by Scorpius Digital Publishing. *Siren Promised* his Bram Stoker Award-nominated novel, written with Jeremy Robert Johnson, was released in 2005. His two book series with Stephen Merritt and Lorelei Shannon, *The Blood of Father Time, Books 1 & 2*, a dark time-travel fantasy, was published by Five Star Books in 2007. Mr. Clark's publishing company, IFD Publishing, has released six books, the most recent of which is a full color book of his artwork, *The Paint in My Blood*. He and his wife, Melody, live in Oregon. For more info visit: www.alanmclark.com

Elizabeth Massie

Two-time Bram Stoker Award-winning author Elizabeth Massie has published 26 novels for adults, teens, and young readers, primarily in the genres of horror, historical fiction, and media tie-ins. Her titles include *Sineater*, *Welcome Back to the Night*, *Wire Mesh Mothers*, *Homeplace*, *The Tudors: King Takes Queen*, *The Tudors: Thy Will Be Done*, and others. She lives in the Shenandoah Valley of Virginia with illustrator Cortney Skinner. She hates cheese and loves World's Softest Socks, and thinks Alan Clark has one wicked sense of humor.

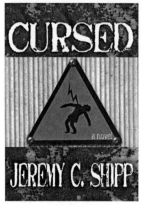

Cursed by Jeremy C. Shipp

hc 978-1-933293-86-8, $29.95, 216p
tpb 978-1-933293-87-5, $14.95, 216p

Your life is no longer recognizable, every detail corrupted by unknown forces. The harder you struggle, the more you suffer. Your words mean nothing, your actions backfire, and one by one everybody you know is sucked down with you. That's because: a) someone or b) something is after you with a vengeance. Even with the help of other cursed people, you don't stand a chance because you're all, you know, cursed.

That means you and everyone you know will:
   1. suffer
   2. die
   3. amuse your tormentor

That is, unless you figure out how to manipulate the person behind this and turn their power against them. Check your list a second time because they're probably on it. The only thing left to do is scratch them off.

Finale by Paul A. Toth

hc 978-1-933293-84-4, $29.95, 164p
tpb 978-1-933293-85-1, $13.95, 164p

When Jonathan Thomas receives a threatening letter apparently sent by an ex-girlfriend, he pursues the sender but finds himself unraveling another mystery he would have better left unsolved. *Finale* tells the story of this wanderer's journey to a faultline deep within himself. The chapters descend from eight to zero as Jonathan travels from his most recent lover to first, finally reaching zero when he leaps into the fissure that divides him. Between lovers, internal "earthquake" chapters rise in magnitude from 1.0 to 8.0.

The lovers include: Mary Whitcomb, a Zelda Fitzgerald double now selling endangered turtle eggs; Azal, who forces Jonathan to visit her father's grave wearing the dead man's clothes; Kerrie, ex-speedfreak and comic book junky; and Holly, who invites Jonathan and the other lovers to his "funeral." Will the funeral startle Jonathan out of self-deception, or lead to knowledge he never should have gained?

CPSIA information can be obtained at www.ICGtesting.com
Printed in the USA
LVOW132057261212

313225LV00002B/629/P